F

BLACK RIDER

BLACK RIDER

Jackson Cole

Chivers Press • **Thorndike Press**
Bath, England **Waterville, Maine USA**

This Large Print edition is published by Chivers Press, England, and by Thorndike Press, USA.

Published in 2002 in the U.K. by arrangement with the author c/o Golden West Literary Agency.

Published in 2002 in the U.S. by arrangement with Golden West Literary Agency.

U.K. Hardcover ISBN 0–7540–7448–X (Chivers Large Print)
U.K. Softcover ISBN 0–7540–7449–8 (Camden Large Print)
U.S. Softcover ISBN 0–7862–4485–2 (Nightingale Series Edition)

The text of this Large Print edition is unabridged.
Other aspects of the book may vary from the original edition.

Set in 16 pt. New Times Roman.

Printed in Great Britain on acid-free paper.

British Library Cataloguing in Publication Data available

Library of Congress Cataloging-in-Publication Data

Cole, Jackson.
    Black rider / by Jackson Cole.
        p. cm.
    ISBN 0–7862–4485–2 (lg. print : sc : alk. paper)
    1. Texas Rangers—Fiction. 2. Texas—Fiction. 3. Large type books. I. Title.
    PS3505.O2685 B56 2002
    813'.54—dc21
                                                    2002071997

CHAPTER ONE

THE SILVER STAR

'How come you figger you got the makin's of a Ranger, son?'

Stern old Captain Tom McDonough's voice was not unkind. He liked the looks of the young cowboy who stood before his desk, liked his great height, the sweep of his broad shoulders and deep chest that swelled up from his sinewy waist. He liked also the lean bronzed face with its slightly wide, good-humored mouth, high-bridged nose and broad, thoughtful forehead topped by thick black hair.

It was the eyes of the man that intrigued Captain Tom, however. They were slightly long, set deep beneath level black brows, the lashes black and heavy. Their color was a smoky gray-green. They reminded the old Ranger captain of other eyes he had seen—the eyes of men who made history in the old West, in whose presence other men spoke softly and moved their hands with care.

'John Ringo had eyes like that,' mused the captain, 'and Doc Holliday, and Wyatt Earp. This young feller is the kind what has in him the makin's of a Ringo or a Holliday if he'd happen to get off to the wrong start, and the

1

makin's of a fust class peace officer, or I'm mistook.' Aloud he repeated his question—

'How come you figger you got the makin's of a Ranger?'

Walt Lee smiled down at the old captain from his great height and his green eyes were suddenly sunny as a summer sea.

'I know I got the hankerin',' he chuckled.

'That's somethin',' admitted the captain. 'You say you been workin' for Samp Burley? I know Samp; he us'ally hires goods hands. How's things over to the Lazy B?'

'Not so good as they might be,' Walt replied. 'Been havin' a mite of rustler trouble of late. Seems wideloopin' is sorta on the prod hereabouts. Calculate we been gettin' the wrong sorta folks in this section. That's one reason I'd like to get on with the Rangers,' he admitted. 'I sorta hanker to get a whack at certain gents I can call to mind.'

Captain McDonough pulled his grizzled moustache. Suddenly he glanced up, a gleam in his frosty old eyes.

'Ever hear of Wolf Felton?' he asked suddenly.

Walt Lee's lean jaw tightened and his green eyes turned cold as gray moonlight sifting through whirling snow.

'Yes, suh,' he replied briefly.

'What you know 'bout him?' challenged Captain Tom.

'Nothin' more for shore than what ev'body

else knows,' Walt answered. 'He owns a ranch and cattle and hires a passel of long-haired salty jiggers. Folks say he usta be one of Quantrell's guerrillas, but I can't say as to that.'

Captain McDonough nodded. He liked the moderation of the cowboy's reply. Captain Tom knew that Walt was familiar with the other things people said about Felton.

Yes, Bruce Felton owned a ranch, and cattle. He also owned a reputation that was not envied by decent cattlemen. So far, however, he had always managed to keep at least in that shadowy twilight-land between honest ranching and downright outlawry. People suspected Felton, but were never able to prove anything.

'Ever run up 'gainst him?' asked the captain.

'Not d'rect,' Walt replied. 'His spread laps ours. We been missin' quite a few dogies of late,' he added with meaning.

Captain Tom nodded. 'The Rangers has been sorta int'rested in Felton,' he announced, 'but he's smooth, if he *is* crooked. He knows our boys and is allus on the lookout for 'em. Ev'thin's hunky-dory when any of 'em shows up.

'You're still workin' for Burley?' he asked suddenly.

'Yeah,' Walt nodded. 'I couldn't quit Samp offhand, he's been too square with me. I'm boss of the trail herd what's headin' for

3

Concha, the railroad town, t'morrer.'

'You keep on workin' for Samp, for a spell,' said the Captain, 'but listen—'

His stern old eyes bored into the cowboy's.

'A puncher with no Ranger c'nections might git the lowdown on Felton,' he suggested softly.

Walt nodded. 'I think I understand, suh.'

Captain Tom opened the drawer of his desk. He took out a shining silver star set on a silver circle, the famous star of the Rangers, the badge of the Frontier Battalion.

'This jigger ain't got nobody pinned to it,' he remarked cryptically. 'It's waitin' for somebody to come 'long what's hefty enough to hold it up. Don't forget what I said 'bout Felton, son.'

Walt shook hands and bade the Captain goodbye. McDonough chuckled as he gazed after his tall form.

'I got a notion that star ain't gonna stay lonesome over long,' he declared.

CHAPTER TWO

STAMPEDE

It was *night*. The gaunt crag-fingers of the western Tonto Hills had pulled down the moon and drowned her in the flood of her own silver tears. The stars burned the high Texas

4

sky like needle points in a black velvet robe. Borne on the wings of a pale wind flitting ghostlike across the Mesa came a low murmur that grew to a grumble, a rising roar. New stars flashed against the eastern sky—golden stars that flung up widely, sparkled for an instant and vanished. A sudden red glow beat back the shadows and bloodied the smoke-trees and the grasses. An eerie wail silenced the coyotes for a shivering moment. The two cowboys who had been resting comfortably sat up in their blankets.

'Tom, she's comin'!'

Walt Lee gazed steadily at the giant eye boring through the night. Tom Williams sat up straighter. Railroad trains were still uncommon enough to be interesting. A steer bawled nervously and Walt cast an anxious glance in the direction of the trail herd.

'She don't pass close enough to scare 'em bad,' said Williams, sensing his thought.

The night rider, Ted Lewis, began to sing:

'Oh, I ain't got no use for the wi-i-i-men!'

Williams snorted his disgust. 'Beef critters sho' are a crazy lot,' he grumbled. 'The idear of anythin' bein' quieted by that racket!'

On came the giant engine, exhaust crashing against the stars, siderods clanging, drivers spinning the roaring miles behind her. Comet-like she flashed past the milling trail herd and on into the west. Rumbling cars, bobbing caboose, glaring red rear markers—the nights swallowed them up.

The herd quieted. The coyotes began anew their mournful yipping. The two tired punchers lay down again.

'This time t'morrer we'll have these ambulatin' beef steaks safe in Concha and off our hands,' grunted Williams, pulling the blanket over his ears.

'Yeah, and I'll be damn glad of it,' said Walt.

The great clock in the sky wheeled on. Walt, sensing it was near time for him to relieve Lewis, stirred in his sleep.

Crash! Crakety-crack-crack!

Walt Lee shot out of his blankets wide awake. Guns were blazing. Men were yelling. Slickers were crackling and snapping. The bawling of terrified cattle provided the high notes. The rumble of their stampeding hoofs the bass.

Walt pawed for his gun belt, snapped it around his waist. He jerked both Colts and ran toward the herd, firing at shadows flickering through the starlight. Pounding after him came Williams.

Looming gigantic against the sky, a rider thundered down upon the two punchers. Walt flung up his gun. His finger curled on the trigger. Then horse and man were blotted out by a terrific blaze of roaring white light. The sky split in two. Black darkness poured past the curling edges and blotted out all things.

Walt Lee opened his eyes to the

6

accompaniment of sickening pain and a steady flow of profanity. The pain came from a long gash just above his right temple. The cuss words came from Tom Williams who sat contemplating the red bandage about his own left leg.

Williams saw the young puncher staring at him and grunted.

'Come to, hey? Figgered you would soon. Heah, take a snort of this.'

He passed Walt a flask. The fiery liquor burned his throat but cleared his head. He sat up, weaving dizzily.

'What the hell happened?' he asked. Williams' reply was terse and to the point—

'They creased you, put a slug through my leg, killed Lewis and wide-looped the trail herd.'

'Killed Lewis! You sho', Tom?'

'Drilled him dead centre. He's layin' over theah 'side that big rock. I crawled to him and saw I couldn't do nothin'. Then I crawled back and washed yore haid and tied it up best I could. Can't stand on this leg.'

Walt climbed slowly to his feet, reeling drunkenly for a moment.

'What you figgerin' on doin'?' Williams asked.

'Put Ted wheah the kiyotes won't get him, fust thing, and then find our bronks; don't callate they strayed far.'

'Over in that grove,' said Williams, jerking

7

his thumb toward the nearby clump of trees. Walt took a step in that direction, stopped.

'Tom, who you reckon did this?'

Williams swore appallingly. 'Wolf Felton, the damned drygulchin' sidewinder! I got a good look at him by gun light jest as I went down. Him and his long-haired hellions!'

Walt wedged Lewis' body in a crevice and covered it with boulders. He stuck the little puncher's gun in his own waistband. Then he caught the horses, saddled them and helped Williams to mount.

'Wheath we goin', Walt?' the old puncher asked.

'To Concha,' Walt told him briefly, 'that leg of yores needs a doctor.'

'And,' he added, 'Felton'll take them dogies to Concha. He knows the railroad's waitin' for 'em and's payin' a top price. Felton'll claim they're his own; but I ain't gonna let him get away with it.'

Williams stared. 'Walt,' he protested, 'theah ain't nothin' you can do; them cattle ain't branded. Felton'll have his men theah and ev'ry damn one of them'll swear they're Felton cattle.'

'And I'll swear they ain't,' said Walt Lee. Williams shook his head in wordless dismay.

Concha, the hell-town the C. & P. railroad construction forces had built! Lee and Williams reached it just as dusk was falling. Old Tom was very sick and Walt was in little

8

better shape. As they rode down the main street, things seemed vague and unreal. Their eyes were dazzled by the blaze of light. Their ears hummed with the noisy turmoil all about them. Men with gold in their pockets and the passions of red blood and lusty life in their hearts shouted and sang. The shrill laughter of women coiled nervously about the whine of fiddles and the beat of guitars. Feet scraped and shuffled. Cards whispered stealthily one against another. Dice clicked. Roulette wheels hummed. Bottle necks chinked against glass.

Walt leaned from his saddle and halted a man who was shuffling along the middle of the road.

'Wheah can I find a doctor?' he asked. The man gazed at his red eyes and snorted.

'Doctor, hell! Don't need no doctors in this town—jest undertakers!'

Despite the pain in his wounded head, Walt chuckled. He danced about, saw a hitch rack in front of a blaring saloon.

'C'mon,' he said to Williams, 'we'll leave the cayuses heah and get a drink. Mebbe the barkeep can tell us wheah a sawbones is— barkeeps knows everythin'.'

Leaning heavily on Walt's shoulder, Williams managed to hobble to the bar. They downed raw whiskey in wryfaced gulps. Walt questioned the bartender.

'Jest 'round the next corner is Doc McChesney's office,' the drink juggler said.

9

Then in answer to another question:

'Railroad headquarters? End of this street. Board shack set under a cottonwood is Barrington's office; he's the Big Boss.'

Walt left Williams in the care of Doc McChesney, refusing to have his own wound dressed. He stumbled down the main street, jostled by drunken railroaders, cowboys, miners. Women with flaming cheeks and lips leered at him from eyes that were hawklike for all their brightness. Some spoke to him. Others plucked at the sleeve of his dusty shirt. He shook them off, shouldered the men aside and lurched on toward where the darkness of the prairie beat like a sable wall against the glare of the lights. He reached the shack that housed Superintendent Barrington, flung the door open without knocking and entered.

Two men were seated at a long table. One, a grizzled giant with the eyes and beak of an eagle, was counting money onto the table. The other, his dead, black eyes following every move of the huge hands that checked the stacks of gold pieces, was lean and stringy with wide, sloping shoulders and hands that were like spear points. Both men looked up as the door opened.

'Felton, you damn cow thief!'

Walt Lee spat the words through his teeth. His gray eyes, burning feverishly, clashed with the lean man's baleful black glare, held it, turned it aside. Wolf Fenton's gun flashed across the table top.

But quick as he was, the big man opposite him was quicker. One huge hand closed on Felton's wrist. The six dropped from nerveless fingers. Felton squalled with pain.

'Theah isn't gonna be any gun play in this office till I know what it's all about!'

The voice that spoke the words was like thunder rolling down a tunnel. It drowned Felton's yowl and silenced Walt. 'Rawhidin' Dave' Barrington, superintendent of the Mountain Division and general superintendent in charge of construction for the C. & P. railroad, glared from one to the other.

'Young man, what was the occasion for that remark of yores?' he demanded of Walt.

Walt told him the story of the night before. Felton listened with a sneer on his thick lips and when Walt had finished he laughed sarcastically.

'Been eatin' loco weed or jest plain crazy,' he scoffed. 'Mr. Barrington, I got a dozen men heah in town what can swear them steers came direct from my ranch. I can prove I was right heah in Concha the time this feller says somebody widelooped his dogies.'

'Tom Williams recognized you, Felton,' Walt said coldly, 'and ev'body in Cochise county knows Tom Williams ain't no liar.'

'Tom Williams can make mistakes same as anybody else!'

'He didn't make no mistake this time!'

11

Superintendent Barrington swore angrily. 'If we didn't need beef so damn bad I'd tell you both to get the hell outa heah and take your damn cattle with you!' he declared. 'You men have gotta settle this thing between you some way, and quick!'

There was finality in the big super's voice. Walt and Felton both recognized it. The latter eyed the young puncher shrewdly, noting the utter weariness that sagged his wide shoulders and lined his bronzed face. Lee was on the verge of exhaustion, his hands were shaking, his movements unsure. Felton arrived at a decision and smiled evilly.

'Them cattle is mine,' he said, 'and I'm plumb willin' to fight for 'em. If this heah jigger is so plumb sartain his rope fits 'em we'll jest shoot it out and the man what leaves on his feet takes the herd. Fair prop'sition?'

Walt read Felton like a book. So did Barrington, no doubt, but he remained silent. Walt nodded slowly.

'Yeah, I un'stand, Felton,' he said. 'You got a rep'tation for bein' almighty fast with a gun. Mebbe I'm as fast as you—chances are I ain't—even when I'm feelin' good. Right now I couldn't shade a sheep herder with creepin' paralysis.'

Felton laughed sneeringly. 'Guess one alibi is good as another. Well—'

'Shut up till I finish, you mangy kiyote!' Walt blazed at him. 'Yore s'posed to be a bad

12

man! Well, I'm gonna see jest how much guts you got. We're gonna shoot it out, Felton, but we're gonna shoot it out in a way what'll give me as good a chance as you. Heah!'

A heavy Colt crashed on the table beside the one Barrington had wrenched from Felton's hand. Felton started back nervously, his eyes slitted with suspicion.

'Mr. Barrington,' Walt said, 'you unload them hawglegs, if you don't mind. Then go into the next room and put a ca'tridge in the barrel of one of 'em—*jest one ca'tridge in* one gun. Then put the guns in a sack and bring 'em both out heah again.'

Grinning like the devil over a sinner, Rawhidin' Dave rose to his feet and picked up the Colts.

'What the hell you up to?' demanded Felton as the super vanished through the inner door.

'You'll find out soon enough,' Walt told him.

Barrington reappeared and dropped a gunny sack on the table.

'All set to go,' he rumbled.

Walt Lee sat down in the chair the super had vacated and faced Wolf Felton across the table.

'All right, *muy malo hombre*,' he drawled, 'reach in the sack and haul out yore weapon. Mebbe you'll get the loaded one, mebbe you won't. When Mr. Barrington counts three we'll shoot it out—across the table. The man who

13

draws the *right gun* is gonna walk away on his feet, *the other ain't!*'

The 'very bad man' wet his lips with a tongue that suddenly felt like a piece of dry leather. He glared at Barrington. The big superintendent's face was inscrutable. Walt Lee's gray eyes mocked him from across the table. With a shaking hand he fumbled the gunny sack, drew out a gun. He cursed viciously when he saw it was not his own.

'Jest as much chance of that one bein' loaded as the other one,' Walt told him, flipping the remaining Colt free. 'All right, Mr. Barrington, start countin'.'

Wolf Fenton stared at the black muzzle scant inches from his face. He raised his own weapon jerkily. It wavered in spite of his efforts to steady it.

'*One!*' boomed Barrington.

Felton jerked convulsively. Sweat was streaming down his face. His eyes were wild and staring.

'Don't cock yore gun till I say "three",' cautioned Barrington. 'Theah's plenty of time; speed don't count for much in this arg'ment.'

Felton drew a deep, shuddering breath and tried to control his shaking hand.

'*Two!*'

Again Felton jerked. He half rose in his chair, slumped back limply and seemed to shrink in size. Walt Lee tensed. His eyes glinted along the long barrel that held steady

14

as a rock.

'Three!'

Felton screamed like an animal in pain, dropped the gun and dived madly for the door. The thud of running feet died quickly in the distance.

Walt Lee sighed deeply and laid his own Colt on the table. He picked up the weapon Felton dropped, spun the cylinder and glanced at it. Then he turned to Barrington.

'Yeah, he had the loaded one!'

Barrington grunted. 'Uh-huh, but he *didn't* have the guts! But you've made a bad enemy, boy, one that won't forget. Well, guess I'd better finish countin' this money.'

Walt rose to his feet. 'I'll hafta hustle out and see Felton don't run that herd off again.'

'Set down!' chuckled Barrington. 'Them dogies were cut up inter beef steaks an hour ago. Our construction camp is needin' meat mighty bad now. How quick can you bring us another herd?'

CHAPTER THREE

HELL LET LOOSE

Walt stowed the gold in a money belt strapped under his shirt, got his horse and stabled it. Then he went to Doc McChesney's office. He

15

found that Tom Williams had been put to bed in a back room. When Doc had finished dressing his wound, Walt folded his arms on the table, laid his head on them and went to sleep. McChesney, wise in the ways of the plainsmen, did not disturb him. Three hours later Walt awakened feeling pretty good aside from a slight stiffness and soreness. He grinned amiably at Doc who sat reading on the far side of the table.

'I'm plumb starved,' he announced. 'Guess I'll amble out and surround some ham and eggs and look the town over.'

Although it was well after midnight, Concha was wilder than ever. Walt's eyes brightened as the roaring excitement began to filter into his blood. He ate hugely at a Chinaman's restaurant and had several drinks. A poker game held his interest for a while; then he moved on seeking other diversion. A blaring string band drew him through swinging doors into a room none too brightly lighted by two huge swinging lamps.

There was a bar in this room—a big one—but no card games. The shuffle of heavy boots and the click of high French heels beat through the wailing of the string band. Glasses pounded the bar in time to the music. Voices roared the refrain:

'Oh, Susanna, Oh, don't you cry for me—'

16

Walt saw the flash of white shoulders, the billowing of short skirts. He threaded his way through the dancers to the bar.

'Straight whiskey and plenty of it's all we got,' boomed the bartender.

'How you like 'er?' he asked as Walt downed his drink.

'Not so bad,' drawled the puncher, 'sorta like swallerin' a lighted skyrocket. Pour me another one.'

A girl flitted through the dim light and snuggled up against Walt.

'Hiyi, cowboy,' she said, 'who tied your head up for you?'

'I was figgerin' on meetin' you,' Walt grinned, 'and I knowed if you hung yore rope on me I'd get a plumb swelled haid, so I bought a hat three sizes too big and had to wear a rag under it to make it fit.'

'Nice boy! But aren't you going to dance with me?'

Walt glanced down at her. She was small with a flame of red hair, great dark eyes with blue circles under them, thin painted cheeks and a red mouth.

'Why sho', Ma'am, I'd be plumb pleased to,' he replied courteously.

The girl gave him a quick look in which there was something of surprise.

'How old are you?' she asked suddenly.

'Twenty-six, come next January,' Walt smiled. 'Why?'

'Nice boy!' she said slipping into his arms.

The dance was the wild dance of the frontier towns. Brawny arms clasped the girls close, whirling them clear off their slim feet at times. Men who had not seen a woman in months looked at their partners with hot eyes, and the girls looked back, with calculating eyes. Feet pounded the wooden floor. Voices shouted to the musicians to play faster. Somebody began roaring another song.

'The days of old! The days of gold!
The days of Forty-nine!'

'Forty-nine, Hell!' howled a drunken miner. 'Forty-nine ain't gonna be a piddlin' to what we'll see when the road gets across the Enchanted Mesa and inter the Tonto Hills! And it won't be long, gents!'

'This burg'll make Virginia City at her biggest look like a string of *'dobe* shacks!' whooped another.

'When the work's all done this fall!'

The band abruptly changed its tune. Wailing and sobbing, the guitars and violins poured forth the haunting melody of that old, old, lonely song of the Southwest—*La Paloma*:

'If a white dove should come winging . . .'

A Mexican with a voice like golden wine gushing into a crystal goblet began to sing the words. Men dropped their shaggy heads onto white shoulders and sobbed. Some of the girls furtively wiped their eyes. Others laughed jeeringly. Walt felt his partner press closer and closer to him. He smiled down into her dark eyes.

'It's a nice song, Ma'am.'

'Yes, it is!'

Again the music changed. With a wild crash of chords the band leaped into the eerie, shrieking strains of 'The Devil's Dream.'

Faster and faster drummed the guitars. Louder and louder screeched the violins. The music sounded sinister and threatening in the shadowy light, filled with tragedy to come. Men stiffened and glanced warily over their shoulders.

Walt sensed the growing tension. His gaze shifted from his partners's face and roved about the crowded room. Something peculiar in a purposeful grouping about the entrance caught his eye.

'And every damn one of them jiggers has got long hair!' he muttered.

Abruptly he wheeled the girl out of the crowd, steered her to the bar and released her. She looked up at him with puzzled eyes.

'Aren't you going to—' she began, her voice trailing away beneath his regard.

'No Ma'am, I ain't,' he smiled. 'You're too

nice a girl, and I sorta like you. Heah—'

The girl stared at the gold piece in her hand, then back at him.

'It was wuth it—jest to dance with you,' Walt said softly. 'Now run down to the other end of the bar and get yoreself a drink. I'm expectin' some friends any minute now.'

The girl gave him a perplexed look, then did as she was told. Walt leaned against the bar, hands hanging loosely by his sides, watching the entrance from the corner of his eye. The men there had spaced out and were bending searching glances about the room. One spoke something in a low tone. His companions turned to face the bar. Walt saw hands flash down.

His own hands were already down. They came up filled with guns that streamed fire and smoke. Two of the men by the entrance slumped to the floor; but the others glided forward, bending low, peering through the smoke of their own guns.

Bullets drummed into the bar beside Walt. One twitched through his sleeve. Another grazed his cheek. A third man was down, but the others were weaving closer, firing with care.

Walt's left-hand gun suddenly tipped up. Flame gushed from its muzzle.

Crash!

The room grew more shadowy as one of the big hanging lamps flew to fragments.

Crash!

20

Darkness like the inside of a safe swooped down. Through it the yells of men, the screams of women and the roar of guns sounded like Hell let loose for recess. Walt slipped swiftly along the bar and collided with a figure. His gun thrust forward, but a small hand gripped his wrist and a voice sounded in his ear.

'Don't shoot, it's me!'

Walt recognized the little dancing girl. 'This way!' she screamed through the tumult. 'Don't ask questions—just follow me.'

She tugged hard at his wrist and Walt followed her. He passed around the end of the bar and bumped against a wall.

'Cover the doors and winders, boys!' bellowed a voice. 'Don't let the polecat sneak out! Get a light goin', somebody!'

Hinges screeched. The girl tugged frantically. Walt shuffled forward and felt a breath of cooler air. The pandemonium in the dance hall was suddenly deadened to a dull drone. Walt stumbled against a step.

'Up the stairs,' whispered his companion. 'Now to the right. Wait!'

There was a jingle of keys. Walt was tugged forward again. Another door closed. His guide left him.

A light flared, steadied as the chimney was replaced on the kerosene lamp. Walt faced the girl who stood in the middle of a tiny room with curtains closely drawn at the windows.

'This is the last place they'll think of

looking—for a while, anyway,' she said.

'Yore room?' Walt asked. The girl nodded.

'I ain't gonna chance gettin' you inter trouble,' Walt protested.

'You won't,' she assured him. 'I'm going to let you out of the window. You can slip away in the dark.'

She extinguished the lamp. Walt heard her fumbling with the curtains. Pale moonlight filtered into the room.

'It's just a little drop to the ground,' the girl whispered.

Walt strode to the window and looked out. It faced on the back of the dance hall. Everything seemed silent and deserted. He turned to the girl.

'Ma'am,' he said, 'yore a square-shooter, a plumb square-shooter! I won't forget what you done for me tonight.'

Suddenly he caught her in his arms, lifted her off her feet and kissed her painted lips. Then he dropped her lightly to the floor and slipped through the open window.

The little dance-hall girl, the back of one slim hand pressed tightly against her lips, watched him vanish around a corner. For another moment she stood staring at nothing. Then she shrugged her shoulders, patted her hair into place and, hand on swaying hip, sauntered down the stairs and into the roaring dance hall.

Walt wasted no time getting his horse from

the stable. And he wasted no time getting out of town. He did not underestimate Wolf Felton.

'Musta had me trailed an' figgered he had me boxed up in that honky-tonk,' he muttered as he rode swiftly through the dying moonlight. 'Set his long-haired killers onto me, and if it hadn't been for that little *senorita* the chances are they'd have got me. Felton kept outa sight, as usual. Wouldn't be possible to hang a thing on him.'

'What I'm gonna do is hang that higger on the hot end of a bullet some day!' he declared wrathfully a little later.

CHAPTER FOUR

HELL FLAMES HIGH

Old Samp Burley, who owned the Lazy-B and was Walt's boss, cursed until his head was ringed by a sulphur-colored halo.

'Pore little Ted Lewis,' he concluded, 'I knowed his maw and pa both. If I ever get my hands on the side-winder what dropped him—'

Walt drew a heavy Colt from his right-hand holster and laid it on the table. In the plain black walnut grips the initials 'T.L.' were carved.

'I'm packin' Ted's gun now,' he said simply.

23

Old Samp nodded. He knew that grim code of the West: the avenger did his work with his slain friend's gun, if he could. More plainly than threats or promises, that simple statement told him that Walt Lee would never rest until Ted Lewis in his lonely grave could sleep sound in the knowledge that the man who sent him there had got what was coming to him. The ranch owner turned to another subject.

'The boys has got a new trail herd damn near ready, bigger one than the last one, but how the hell we gonna get it to the railroad? Felton'll never get over you makin' him take water that way. He'll be out to cash you in and grab off anythin' we try to sell. We ain't got enough men to fight Felton, Walt.'

Walt sat silent for a moment, then he spoke slowly.

'Nope, Boss, we ain't; but mebbe we got brains enough.'

Burley stared. 'What the hell you got up yore sleeve?" he demanded.

Walt leaned across the table. 'Boss, we ain't got no more chance of deliverin' that herd to Concha by way of the Tonto Trail than a jackrabbit has of lickin' a rattlesnake. We'd just be playin' inter Felton's hands. But listen—I got a idear. The railroad needs beef bad and is willin' to do a lot to get it. 'Sides, I got a notion that big superintendent sorta took a likin' to me and 'cause of that he'll give us

24

the inside track. Now jest 'fore the railroad runs inter Crazy House canyon, it passes mighty close to our south range. Theah's a sidin' and a water tank theah, too. If we could get the railroad to run a train of cars onto that sidin', we could knock t'gether some loadin' pens, hustle the dogies inter the cars and send 'em to Concha and the construction camps hell-whoopin'. Even if Felton is ridin' herd on us and finds out what we're gonna do, he wouldn't have time to get ahead of us.'

Old Samp swore a mighty oath. 'I b'lieve you've hit it!' he declared. 'You think the railroad'll send a train?'

'I'm ridin' to Concha t'morrer to find out.'

'With that haid? You ain't been outa the saddle for four days now.'

'Head's all right—jest scratched,' grunted Walt, 'and I feel better in a saddle than any place else.'

Walt rode around Concha and straight to where the C. & P. was rolling its twin steel ribbons westward. He found Barrington on the job.

'All right,' the big super rumbled terse agreement. 'Have your herd theah on time. I'll have the train.'

Three nights later the Lazy-B hurried their trail herd to the little water-tank siding called Haskel. The train was already there. Rawhidin' Dave Barrington himself was in charge. Loading pens and chutes were quickly thrown

25

together. The wild-eyed, bellowing steers were hustled into the cars.

Walt and two other punchers, Hassayampa Hawkins and Benchleg Bowles, would ride the train to Concha and help with the unloading.

Barrington saw Walt eyeing the big locomotive curiously.

'How'd you like to ride on the engine, boy?' he asked.

'Fine!' Walt exclaimed with enthusiasm. 'I allus did wanta fork one of these rail runnin' cayuses.'

Barrington climbed into the cab, Walt following him closely.

'Hank,' the super told the old engineer, 'you toddle back to the crummy and rest; I'll run her inter Concha. Take that shack with you, too—it's a short train and he ain't needed up heap. That'll give us more room in the cab.'

Hogger and head breakman hurried back to the caboose, glad of a chance to take it easy on the cushions. The two Lazy-B waddies were already there.

'Keep outa the fireman's way,' Barrington told Walt. 'That mainline switch is open, ain't it?' he called to the tallowpot.

'All set to go,' replied the fireman. 'Conductor's wavin' a highball.'

Barrington kicked the cylinder cocks open and cracked the throttle. Walt heard water and steam hiss through the open cocks. The big engine's exhaust boomed wetly, the siderods

26

clanked, the tall drivers turned over slowly, spun with a clash and a roar and then gripped the sanded rails. Barrington eased the short train out of the siding, rolled slowly along until the rear brakeman had closed the switch and swung aboard the caboose.

'Highball!' shouted the fireman.

Barrington widened on the throttle. The exhaust quickened to a crackling purr. The siderods clanged a steady song. The great 452 thundered up the winding grade toward Crazy Horse canyon, twenty miles distant.

Walt Lee, hollow-eyed from lack of sleep, weary from days and nights in the saddle, watched what went on in the cab with keen interest. The skill with which the chunky little tallowpot fed coal into the roaring firebox held him fascinated. He watched him build up a huge hump of coal just inside the door and then send his shovelfuls sliding over it to right and left, straight ahead or, with a skillful flick of his wrist, into the back corners. The fireman threw him a friendly grin.

'Wanta put one in?' he asked.

The tall puncher picked up the shovel uncertainly, and opened the fire door. Blasting heat seared his face. A fierce white glare blinded him. The lurch and sway of the flying engine threw him off balance. The huge shovelful of coal he had scooped up went scattering over the deck. He heard Barrington chuckle.

'Ride 'em, cowboy!' rumbled the big super. 'Yore pullin' leather and I can see daylight 'tween you and the hull!'

Walt teetered about and grimly drove the shovel into the coal.

'Don't take so much on yore scoop,' cautioned the fireman. 'Spread yore feet wider apart and let yore knees go loose. It's jest about the same as ridin' a hoss.'

Walt followed instructions and managed to get a fire in. Barrington nodded approval. The tallowpot was plainly pleased.

Walt persisted at his self appointed task. The skilled fireman saw to it that the steam pressure kept up, but he let the puncher handle the scoop about every other time. Walt was becoming highly interested and much more competent by the time the black loom of Crazy Horse canyon hove into view.

Barrington glanced at his sweaty face and rumbled an order.

'Squat down heah on the deck ' side my seatbox and take it easy a bit; yore liable to make yoreself sick.'

Walt obeyed, leaning his aching back and shoulders against the reverse lever, which Barrington had almost straight-up-and-down.

Towering grim and black, the portals of Crazy Horse canyon blotted out the stars. Barrington dropped the reverse bar a notch or two and widened the throttle a trifle. He leaned far out the window, peering ahead.

Crash! Crash! Crash!

Barrington lunged back, crouching low. The fireman stiffened, a surprised look on his face; then he toppled forward and sprawled across the deck, blood pouring from a gaping wound just over his heart.

Crash! Crash! Crash!

Bullets ripped and stormed through the cab. Walt leaped up and was swept to the deck again by Barrington's great arm.

'Keep down!' barked the super. 'You can't see nothin' to shoot at! We'll be outa range in a minute!'

Around a curve careened the racing engine. Barrington leaped to the seatbox once more, leaned out the window. A quick glance told him the track ahead was clear. He whirled back to Walt, who was bending over the fireman.

'Johnny dead?'

Walt nodded. 'Yeah, drilled plumb centre.'

'Lay what's left of the pore feller heah 'longside my seatbox,' Barrington directed. 'Then grab that shovel—yore done elected to a job, son; lucky you learned somethin' about it. I'll help you keep yore fire in shape, but I can't take my eyes off the track much through this damn canyon.'

Walt shoveled coal. Following Barrington's terse directions, he kept the big engine hot. Fortunately the train was a short one, the locomotive new and in good condition.

29

'Watch out the window when the curve's on yore side,' Barrington shouted. 'Look out for rocks on the track or anythin' that don't look jest right.'

Walt peered ahead, blinking the fire glare out of his eyes. It seemed to persist strangely long, the somber canyon walls ahead kept glowing with it. He suddenly realized he was looking at a genuine light and not an image still filmed on his eyeballs.

'Mr Barrington,' he shouted, 'I b'lieve theah's a fire burnin' somewheah ahead of us!'

The super leaped to the fireman's seatbox, leaned out and squinted across the wide curve they were rounding. He swore bitterly.

'Now I see why they drygulched us back theah,' he snorted. 'They wanted to give us a good scare, even if they couldn't down us all, and keep us busy thinkin' about bullets till they got us in the canyon. Boy, the sidewinders have set fire to the woods. Our steers are liable to be barbecues and us along with 'em 'fore we get to Concha. Drive yore spurs in and hang on, we're goin' away from heah!'

Around the curve and up the straight-away boomed the great engine. The crashing of the exhaust quickened to a steady roar. Flanges screamed madly against the rails. Clots of fire and clouds of black smoke poured from the tall stack.

Slipping, sliding, stumbling on the reeling deck, Walt Lee bailed coal into the raging fire box. Blasting heat seared his face. The blazing white glare made his eyes ache. The shovel handle turned in his sweaty hands. Through the maze of pain and weariness that enveloped him bored Barrington's terse instructions.

'A little more in those back corners! Now a couple of scoops down 'gainst the flue sheet! Build yore hump higher at the door! Don't take so much on yore shovel!'

Walt began to cough. Smoke was rasping his throat and tightening his lungs. He lurched to the seatbox and stuck his head out for a breath of fresh air. His deep inhalation drew more hot smoke into his aching lungs. He shrank back as waves of heat beat against his face.

Fire was raging down the canyon, leaping from bush to bush, running up the trunks of tall trees and exploding in a burst of flame amid the dry twigs of their crests. The canyon lips were slavering blood. The stars were blotted out by rolling black clouds.

'We gotta go through that?' he shouted to Barrington.

'If we don't go through we're gonna think Hell's a cool spot when we get theah!' the super shouted back. 'Steam's droppin'!'

Walt went back to the deck and the shovel. Barrington dared not leave the throttle for an instant: trees were thundering down along the right-of-way; the ties were on fire in places. Walt, peering through his window again, saw a tall pine, flame spouting from root to topmost

31

branch, waver toward the track. Slowly, majestically it leaned lower and lower. The roaring engine flashed past it. The cars with their bawling cargo rumbled by. Suddenly it rushed down, a blazing blast of destruction. Walt, straining his eyes back through the smoke, saw it graze the bobbing caboose and thunder across the track. He drew a deep breath of relief, peered ahead and let out a yell.

'The bridge! The bridge! It's burnin' up!'

A long, wooden trestle spanned Crazy Horse river. From piers to topmost super-structure it was wrapped in flames. Barrington's hand quivered on the airbrake valve for an instant, then dropped. Wide open came the throttle.

With a screaming crash the engine hit the bridge. Walt felt the blazing structure reel and sway. Burning timbers crashed down on the tank top. One slammed against the cab and rolled off amid a shower of sparks. Fire flickered from the roofs of the cattle cars.

'Theah's a slow order on this bridge—thirty miles an hour—we're doin' seventy!' Barrington shouted.

Once the engine lurched sickeningly on a low rail. Walt thought for a terrible instant they were going over into the river; but she held the iron and roared on. A burning brand smashed against the whistle and jammed it open. Its screeching wail added to the turmoil.

Down went the bridge to flaming destruction; but an instant before it fell, the rear wheels of the caboose whipped onto solidly grounded rails.

Blue Hole tunnel yawned blackly. The short train crashed through and screeched to a stop on the far side of the canyon. Trainmen and punchers swarmed over the burning cars, stamping out the flames; drowning them with water drawn from the engine tank. Walt anxiously sought out his two riders and found neither hurt.

'They put so many holes in that darn caboose the road can use it for a sifter,' Benchleg said. 'Knocked some skin off the conductor's arm, too. Say! it's a helluva shame 'bout that pore fireman!'

The cattle train rumbled into Concha with its singed cargo. Johnny Walsh's body was lifted tenderly from the cab and carried away. Walt went to Barrington's office and reckoned the price of the herd.

'That long-haired sidewinder, Felton, is gettin deeper and deeper in my debt all the time,' he told Barrington. 'I liked that fireman.'

'You think it was Felton?'

'Sho'! Who else? But we can't prove a thing. He kept plumb in the clear, as usual. This makes two times. Three's the charm!'

Walt went back to the Lazy-B to get another herd together.

'After this I'll buy from you exclusive, long as you can bring 'em to me,' Barrington had said. 'And tell yore boss the price of beef has riz.'

Old Samp Burley heard the news with great satisfaction, and rode across the Border. There he bought cattle from Mexican *haciendados.* Swarthy *vaqueros* delivered the dogies to the Lazy-B, swapped yarns with their fellow cowboys north of the Line and rode back to their *haciendas.*

'Them Mexican punchers dress sorta fancy but they ain't bad sorts,' was Hassayampa Hawkins' verdict.

'I worked on one of them *haciendas*, once,' said Benchleg Bowles. 'It was a swell big ranch, too. The *haciendado* was a fine old gent who wore velvet pants, a forty-dollar *sombrero* and went bare-footed.'

CHAPTER FIVE

'BRING US MEAT'

The C. & P. continued to build railroad. Her mailed fist shattered the Tonto crags, ripped them apart. Fingers of steel clawed and tore at the stubborn hills. The click of picks, the chatter of steam shovels and the rumble of dynamite routed the silence that had reigned over the desolate wastelands for a thousand centuries. The glaring beams of locomotive headlights beat against the cliffs and frightened the desert owls from their nesting places. Ever the twin steel ribbons rolled westward.

Superintendent Barrington looked over the long communication lines from his base at Concha, frowned and arrived at a decision. He would move Concha!

Move it he did! Forty miles farther west he built his new construction camp. Concha rubbed its eyes, saw the golden harvest of the construction workers going west—and went west too! Concha that was became a ghost town. Coyotes prowled through the deserted dance halls. Bats hung over the silent bars. Gophers chattered where roulette wheels once had clicked and whirred.

But in the shadow of the towering Tonto Hills the new Concha roared as never before. Dance hall girls, gamblers, saloon keepers streamed after the railroaders and set up business before the boards of the huge shacks were fully nailed in place. Whiskey, raw and red, flowed like water. The girls put on new dresses. The gamblers smoothed their black coats, saw that their derringers were loose in their sleeves and donned their best poker faces. The construction workers thronged the streets in search of wine, women and song. Wine in the form of sizzling rotgut they must

35

have, women they would like, song they could put up with. The gamblers filled out a gorgeous quartette that was lusty if not musical.

*'The days of old! The days of gold!
The days of Forty-nine!'*

Rawhidin' Dave Barrington, empire builder, looked about and saw more than a raw frontier shack town. Here was the site for a city. His orders clicked over the wires to distant offices. Concha's roar took on a wilder note.

Ponderous structures built for permanence began rising at the construction camp. Machine shops, roundhouses, mills and factories—all the many things needed at a division point of a great railroad. A vast yard sprawled its steel tentacles across the prairie.

More and more workers poured into Concha; and after them surged the raven host. New dance halls must be built to house fresher faces and brighter eyes. Gamblers with keener wits and more money to risk sat at tables that still smelled of the forests from which they had been hewn. Varied liquors flanked the brawny whiskey jugs in multicolored array.

Concha roared!

Barrington sent an urgent message to Walt Lee. Meat was needed, much meat. How about another trail herd? A big one!

Walt had the cattle ready, plenty of them;

36

but how to get them safe to Concha? Across the Tonto Trail lay the dark shadow of Wolf Felton, twice defeated and more vengeful than ever. Barrington would not risk another train from Haskel. It was up to Walt.

Old Samp Burley called his young foreman to the ranch-house.

'Walt,' he stated, 'I got a idea.'

He spread a rude sketch on the table, tracing the lines with a blunt finger.

'I believe I done figgered somethin' out,' he said. 'Felton's got us blocked north and west over the Tonto Trail; but s'posin' we was to head south inter Mexico, turn east a ways and then travel north 'longside the Tonto Desert? Then we could cut west and come to Concha without ever hittin' the Tonto Trail. That would put a kink in Felton's rope. I done got it all figgered out heah on this paper.'

Walt eyed the sketched route dubiously. 'It's one helluva long drive,' he objected. 'It'll run all the fat off the beef critters, even if we manage to get 'em to Concha that way. The Tonto Desert ain't no picnic grounds and when we head west we'll hafta cut across a section of *El Infierno Negro*. The Black Hell's no place to drive cattle through, Boss. 'Sides, we'd hafta swim 'em across Silver River, and if she happens to be on a rampage that won't be easy. No, I don't like it.'

'But it's a chance,' urged Burley. 'You admit we ain't got no chance drivin' over the Tonto

37

Trail with Felton on the prod. Let's give her a whirl, Walt.'

'All right,' Walt agreed reluctantly. 'What you say goes, but I ain't guaranteein' no results.'

'Don't expect you to,' Burley said. 'It's a gamble, and mebbe we'll win.'

Walt rose to his feet. 'I'll try it,' he decided, 'but I ain't gonna take the whole herd. Jest a little bunch to try it out the fust time. Too many dogies in that herd to lose all at once.'

The trip to Mexico and through the hills of Sonora did not trouble Walt. It was a hard drive, but nothing to worry about. But when the purple mountains dropped behind and the herd turned north, the Lazy-B foreman's face became anxious. A long stretch of rugged country confronted him, and before the threats of the Tonto Desert and The Black Hell were met there was the still greater threat of Silver River.

On the afternoon of the sixth day out they arrived on the bank of the stream. Walt gazed at the swirling water and swore disgustedly.

Silver River was not silvery today. It was a tawny flood flecked with fallen trees, water-soaked logs and other odds and ends of flood rubbish. One of the furious mountain storms had poured vast quantities of water into the upper branches of the river.

'Well, it can't be helped,' Walt told his punchers. 'We'll hafta chance it. I *have* crossed

38

this darn ground-travellin' rain storm when she was wuss than this. But I didn't get no fun outa it,' he admitted. 'All right, start 'em in.'

The cattle didn't want to enter the water. They bawled protest, milled and sidled. The punchers used voice and quirt and slicer until their throats were dry and their arms aching. Finally the pressure of those behind prodded the leaders into the stream. They floundered through the shallows, leaning against the current. Soon they were swimming.

The cowboys swam their horses beside and behind the herd, holding it in line, heading it on a long upstream diagonal toward the far bank. Walt Lee strode along the water's edge, watchful of eye, ready to lend a hand where it was most needed.

Without warning disaster struck. A huge uprooted tree came rolling down the current, its shredded branches thrashing, its roots writhing and trailing like the arms of an octopus. A steer was caught in the mess and swept beneath the surface, bawling with terror. Its strangled bleats frightened the others and started them floundering. The punchers urged their horses toward the point of trouble.

Down came the tree, rolling swiftly. A huge limb whipped down upon young Hassayampa Hawkins' horse, knocked the animal off balance and hurled Hassayampa from the saddle. The horse kicked and plunged, dived beneath the welter of branches and headed for the shore.

Walt Lee saw a brown hand break surface, clutch at a thrashing branch and slip off. The sunlight glinted for an instant on a golden head that vanished swiftly. Walt had a cold feeling that that golden head never would be gray. He knew that Hassayampa could not swim a stroke. The tree rolled on the hapless puncher caught in its meshes.

Walt drove his spurs home and rode madly along the bank. He shucked his gun belt as he rode, sent his hat spinning. Where the bank jutted out high over the water he hurled himself from the saddle. He jerked off his heavy 'shotgun' chaps and spurs; but there was no time to remove his tight-fitting boots. Almost fully clothed he dived into the stream and swam toward the rolling tree.

It looked like plain suicide to dare that wild tangle of waterlogged wood. The river swirled and foamed about it. The huge branches came down like rushing pile drivers. One grazed Walt's shoulder and drove him far beneath the surface. He came up sputtering and gasping, in the very heart of the mass.

Hassayampa was wedged in a crotch and as the tree turned he was dragged beneath the surface again and again. He was unconscious when Walt reached him, white and limp.

Walt gripped the flaccid body and tried to drag it free. The rolling trunk took him under, spun him slowly through the air and under again.

'I'll be damned if this ain't wuss than forkin' a mill wheel!' he gulped disgustedly as he went under for the third time.

The tree hit a rock or another water-soaked log. The shock hurled Walt under again, but it also freed Hassayampa. Clutching the half-drowned puncher's collar, Walt dived deeply. He came up clear of the branches and set out with the last of his strength for the shore.

'Heah, let me give you a hand,' sounded a voice beside him.

Benchleg Bowies was swimming his horse, one hand resting lightly on the saddle. He got a grip on Hassayampa and left Walt free to look out for himself. A few minutes later all three were safe on the far bank.

Walt was content to stretch out on the grass and rest while the other riders got the water out of Hassayampa. The yellow-haired puncher finally came around and for a while was decidedly sick. Later he raised himself on a weak elbow, swore feebly and grinned at Walt.

That grin said everything that the undemonstrative plainsman was unable to put into words. Walt grinned back.

'Why the hell can't you pick a time we're not so damn busy to go swimmin'?' he demanded.

Hassayampa rubbed his wet head.

'Say!' he wailed, 'you mean to tell me you didn't bring my hat out, too? Why you long-legged jughead, that hat set me back twenty-seven dollars!'

Walt ruefully regarded what was left of his trail herd. During the confusion more than half of the dogies had been swept down stream and lost.

'I knowed it!' he growled. 'And we got the Tonto Desert and The Black Hell ahead of us yet. We ain't gonna get to Concha with enough beef to make a sandwich!'

It was not quite that bad, but it was bad enough. The Tonto Desert took a toll. So did *El Infierno Negro*. The steers Walt finally delivered to Rawhidin' Dave were gaunt and stringy and few in number.

Barrington was glad to get them, though, even as they were.

'Fresh meat is our biggest trouble right now,' he told Walt. 'We've done cleaned the small ranches around heah, and 'fore I'll buy from Felton I'll make the boys eat *fricaseéd* rattlesnake and horned toad stew. Looks like it's up to yore Lazy-B ranch—it's the only big one 'round heah outside of Felton's. I been tryin' hard to get the Gov'ment to send a troop escort from the fort, but they ain't nothin' come of it as yet.'

Walt's lean jaw set grimly. 'I'll get them gentlemen-cows heah if I hafta graft jaybirdwings on 'em and bring 'em by air!' he declared. 'Say this *pieblo* seems exter woolly t'night.'

42

'Payday,' Barrington explained. 'You'll see things t'night if you hang around.'

Walt Lee saw things in Concha that mad night that he preferred not to remember. He saw wounded men dragging themselves to the uncertain shelter of doorways, dead men lying stark in the streets. He saw women with the eyes of hungry hawks rifling their pockets. He saw men who had been friends fighting together like beats—gouging, tearing, ripping each other's flesh with nails and teeth. Spilled whiskey and spilled blood stained the bars. Gold that was blackened with the sweat of heart-crushing toil flowed across the green tables into the hands of cold-eyed gamblers who never gave their dupes a chance. Fury and lust and greed walked arm-in-arm. Kipling had not yet written—

'There's never a law of God or man runs north of Fifty-Three!'

—but the thought and the sentiment applied well to Concha that night.

Walt rode back to the Lazy-B wracking his brain for a solution of the problem that had been laid before him. Burley had secured still more cattle and the trail herd was larger than when the ill-advised trip by way of Mexico had started. How to get them to Concha? That was the question.

CHAPTER SIX

GOLD!

And then one evening, just at dusk, a man waving a buckskin sack spurred a foaming horse down Concha's main street. Through the wide door of a dance hall he rode the plunging cayuse, scattering the dancers right and left. Women screamed. Men shouted angrily. But the rider heeded none of them. Straight to the bar he thundered. He leaned in the saddle, up-ended the sack and dumped its contents on the gleaming surface.

Dull yellowish lumps! Coarse dust like sun motes under the lights! The man straightened in his saddle and waved the empty sack over his head.

'Gold!' he bellowed. *Gold in the Tonto Hills!'*

Men crowded forward, licking their dry lips. The girls stared with wide, greedy eyes at the yellow heap.

'The best claims ain't been staked!' whooped the man on horseback.

Men glared at each other, fingering the heavy nuggets. There arose a sudden howl like wolves at a kill—and the stampede was on!

Shouting and cursing, men hurled their clinging partners from them and surged to the doors. The rider laughed insanely, knocked the neck off a bottle of wine and tried to make his horse drink it. A bartender gathered up the gold with shaking hands and held it up to him.

'Keep it!' yelled the man. 'I got plenty more! Drinks for the house!'

'The days of old! The days of gold!
The days of Forty-nine!'

Concha had roared. Now Concha thundered, shrieked and howled. The night was a bedlam of shouting, screaming, cursing.

The news spread like wildfire. The streets were crowded. Mounted men raced westward, scattering the crowds like chaff. Bartenders flung away their aprons. Cold-eyed gamblers, with eyes that were cold no longer, jerked off their stiff bosoms and donned woolen shirts. Women, their painted faces clashing hideously with the buckskins and corduroys they wore, joined the exodus.

Gold! Gold! Gold!

It was on every tongue! It was in the very air! The Tonto Hills, sinister in the moonlight, looked down and seemed to smile in grim mockery. But the treasure seekers, heedless of their cold menace, rushed westward.

'Oh, Susanna! Oh, don't you weep for me!'

The madness gripped the construction

45

camp. Workers dropped their tools, packed grub sacks and hurried into the hills. The tall derricks swung idle. The giant engines hissed their displeasure at this enforced idleness. Picks and shovels and bars and gauges gathered rust.

Superintendent Barrington cursed all the fates and schooled his turbulent soul to patience. He knew that it was but a matter of time until his toilers drifted back, glad to discard the problematical gleanings of the hills in favor of the certain gold of payday. With the skeleton staff left him he proceeded to get things in shape against their return.

To this scene of listless activity rode Walt Lee. He grinned at Barrington's sulphurous comments. His life spent amid the Arizona hills and deserts, gold rushes were no novelty to him. His keen mind saw a chance to make capital of the situation.

'Yeah, bring every damn steer you can,' Barrington told him. 'Theah'll be a mighty hungry outfit headin' back this way 'fore long. I know them hills. You eat seldom and slim up theah.'

Walt laughed. 'Well, guess I'll amble inter town and see what's goin' on—that is if the *pueblo* ain't plumb dead and gone to seed.'

'Oh, she's still sorta lively,' Barrington reassured him. 'Most of the girls are still left, and the gamblers, and some of the rum sellers. Not many of my enginemen and trainmen joined the rush, either. T'day was payday, too, for them what was heah to get it. And cowboys have been ridin' in all day. I callate you can get a little action for yore money.'

Walt rode to Concha, stabled his horse and entered a restaurant. He found the place crowded with Slash-K and T-Bar-W punchers who greeted him as a long lost brother. In a compact group they strolled down the main street, which was far from dead-and-gone to seed. They drank heartily and variedly, gathering enthusiasm as they gathered alcohol. Toward midnight they jingled into a combination dance-and-gambling hall.

Wide hat cocked jauntily over one eye, Walt took the scene in. Suddenly he stiffened, his smiling mouth straightened out, his gray eyes glittered.

Seated at one of the poker tables was Wolf Felton. Nearby lounged several of his long-haired gunmen. And seated close to Felton, following his play with avid interest, was the little red-headed dancer who had rescued Walt that hectic night in old Concha.

A hot anger sent the blood pounding to Walt's temples. His feeling toward the girl was nothing more than one of friendly gratitude, but it irked him to see her there beside Felton. He resented the swarthy ranch owner's possessive attitude. Abruptly he strode forward, the Slash-K and T-Bar-W cowboys hostling at his heels.

47

Felton glanced up, recognized Walt. His face went black and he half rose from his chair.

Walt smiled thinly. 'Nope, not t'night, Felton,' he drawled. 'Yore gang ain't half salty enough to try a showdown with this outfit behind me. Make a move and it'll be jest you and me, Felton, jest you and me. You won't have no help.'

Felton relaxed, glowering. The quiet-voiced dealer spoke.

'Any of you gentlemen care to sit in? There are two vacant chairs?'

'Guess I'll try it a whirl,' Walt said. 'You fellers mind hangin' 'round a bit?' he flung over his shoulder.

'Ride 'em, cowboy!' one of the waddies voiced the sentiment of the group. 'We'll be right heah to back yore play if you need us.'

Walt placed gold before him and play at the table resumed. What had been a listless game suddenly grew tense. The others players, noticing the ill feeling between Felton and the tall puncher, sensed impending events. They stiffened, played closer to their vests.

Felton had been the big winner when Walt sat down. Now he started to lose. His scowl grew blacker. His cruel mouth thinned and straightened. Walt smiled mockingly and raked in a hefty pot.

'I bluffed you outa that one, Felton,' he drawled, throwing down a busted flush. 'You had the cards, but you didn't have the guts—jest like the last time we played t'gether.'

Felton's eyes were venomous. 'Play the game and don't gab so damn much!' he spat. Walt chuckled and called for a new deck.

The play quickened; the bets increased. Player after player dropped out until only Walt and Felton faced each other across the green cloth. Silence settled like a blanket.

The dealer flipped the pasteboards. Felton glanced at his hand.

'I'm standin' pat.' He grunted surlily, trying to hide the exultation in his voice.

Walt picked up his cards, hesitated, separated two cards from the others and then seemed to change his mind.

'I'll take one,' he said, dropping the middle card onto the table.

Felton glanced up quickly with narrowed eyes. 'Holdin' two pair and tryin' to draw to make a full house,' was his natural reasoning. He peeped again at his own hand and bet heavily.

Walt hesitated, glanced at his own hand once more and raised. Felton promptly raised him back. Walt regarded him speculatively.

'Got a little flush, eh, Felton?' he said. 'Or mebbe it's a straight. Then again mebbe it's a full house. Well, I'm takin' a chance. I h'ist her twenty more.'

Felton shoved his whole stack of gold forward. 'It goes as it lays,' he growled.

The quiet dealer counted the money. Walt took enough from his own pile to cover the raise.

'I'm seein' you, Felton,' he said.

Felton smirked and spread his cards on the table.

'Nothin' but a little full house, ace-high,' he shrilled, and reached for the pot.

Walt shoved the grasping hand back. 'Jest a minute,' he drawled. 'I didn't have two pair like you figgered, Felton. I throwed away a king, and darned if I didn't catch another one in place of it. But I didn't care, Felton, you see what I held onto was jest *four little deuces!*'

Felton glared at a flock of two-spots spread before his eyes. He cursed viciously and his hate-filled eyes seemed to spit black flame at the smiling cowboy. His men fiddled nervously. The punchers grouped behind Walt moved forward a step.

But Felton was not looking for trouble. He rose to his feet, glowering.

'That cleans me!' he growled.

Walt looked up at him with mocking eyes. He cared nothing for the money he had won, but he was seething with a desire to further humiliate Felton.

'Hol' on a minute, Wolf,' he said softly. 'Tell you what I'll do—The little lady theah 'side you looks sorta good to me. I'll jest play you the whole pile on the table 'gainst her, one hand of showdown.'

50

Felton stared in astonishment. That heap of gold against a dance hall girl who was for sale to anyone for a twentieth part of the sum. Then he understood Walt's meaning and his face grew more furious than ever. He hesitated, dreading to accept the challenge and yet not daring to refuse it.

'Deal!' he said thickly, dropping into his chair again.

Swiftly the dealer flicked the cards. Walt, still smiling mockingly, turned his hand face up. Felton glanced at it and gave a yell of delight.

'Beat you, damn you! I got three sevens and you ain't got a pair!'

Walt nodded and rose to his feet. The little dancer suddenly slipped from her stool and swayed around the table. She placed a slim hand on Walt's arm; her voice rang clearly through the room:

'Come on, cowboy, and buy me a drink. I'd rather trail along with a good loser any time than with a bad winner!'

The punchers let out a jubilant howl. Felton gasped like a strangled fish, half rose in his chair and sank back again, his face a dirty white.

CHAPTER SEVEN

AMBUSH!

Walt rode back to the Lazy-B, a plan seething in his brain. He called the Lazy-B riders into consultation and proceeded to put the plan into effect.

Dawn, in scarlet and gold and emerald and topaz, broke over The Enchanted Mesa. The craggy spires of the Tonto Hills were silver and saffron crowning the deepest purple. A wind like violin notes through rain fluttered the prairie roses. A liquid bird note thrilled farewell to the paling stars.

Down the dusty trail from the Lazy-B ranchhouse cantered the Lazy-B riders. Walt Lee, Tom Williams, still slightly lame, Hassayampa Hawkins, Benchleg Bowles and five more rum punishers. Blankets and plump grub sacks bulked behind their saddles. Two lead pack horses loaded with picks and shovels and other odds and ends of prospecting paraphernalia tugged at their ropes. The punchers were chattering with excitement.

They rode in to Concha, ate heavily and drank, not so heavily. Loudly they discussed their plans with anybody willing to listen.

'To hell with ridin' for forty-per and tough steaks!' yowled Benchleg Bowles, his handlebar moustache bristling across his red face. 'We're gonna scratch a month's pay outa the ground every day. I allus knowed theah was gold in them thar hills. I was a damn fool not to go lookin' for it long ago. Drink deep, you jugheads, money's gonna be a burden from now on!'

'Anybody seen Wolf Felton 'round heah?' Walt Lee asked. 'I'd like to pistol-whip that mangy kiyote once 'fore I head inter the hills. May be gone a long time and somebody's liable to beat me to it 'fore I get back.'

A bartender whispered behind his hand to a fellow worker.

'Lee's drunk as hell on liquor and gold excitement. I've knowed him ten heahs and that's the fust time I ever heard him brag or make a threat.'

The other nodded wisely. 'That yaller stuff does funny things to fellers. Sackful of double-eagles won't kick up no excitement; but a little smatherin' of dust or raw nuggets!—say, I wonder if theah's any chance to buy a hoss and a prospectin' outfit 'round heah now?'

Many of the first exodus had straggled back, sadder if not wiser, and Concha's roar was beginning to deepen when the Lazy-B outfit rode out of town. Walt Lee turned in his saddle, eyed the huddle of ugly yellow shacks and the crowded main street fogging with dust and splashed with color. He smiled thinly and faced ahead toward where the Tonto Hills loomed darkly menacing, but clean and cold and washed in the golden sunshine. He shrugged his shoulders as does a man who drops from them a distasteful garment. His companions had grown silent, their eyes were purposeful.

Dusk found them enveloped by the hills. They made a fire, ate heartily of provisions taken from their saddle bags. Then they dropped worn blankets that had outlived their usefulness, kicked aside old grub sacks that were neatly plumped out with straw and relieved the pack horses of their worthless assortment of junk.

'Mebbe it worked and mebbe it didn't,' Walt said. 'We fooled Concha all right, but somehow I got a hunch we ain't foolin' Felton wuth a cent.'

'What the hell's the good of all this heah hard work we done, then?' complained Hassayampa.

'Jest this,' Walt told him. 'Felton's gonna think he's foolin' us. Stead of swoopin' down on us with all his men, he's gonna fix up a nice little ambushin' somewheah. What we gotta do is outsmart him.'

'But how?' Williams demanded.

'Figger out wheah he's most liable to set his trap, then get the jump on him and smash him 'fore he knows what it's all about.'

Benchleg Bowies snorted. 'Sounds nice, but whether it's gonna *be* nice is somethin' else

54

again.'

With loose rein and busy spur they rode south, veering gradually toward the east. In the dark hours before the dawn they clattered up to the Lazy-B ranch-house.

Old Samp had hot food and steaming coffee ready for them. They wolfed a meal while the wranglers were getting them fresh horses. Then they started the sleepy, rebellious trail herd toward Concha.

Morning came, gray and threatening, but by mid-afternoon the sun was shining brightly. The cowboys were powdered with white dust. The cattle were tired and nervous. Ahead, dipping into hollows, vanishing over hill tops, wound the Tonto Trail, silent and deserted.

Walt Lee peered with puckered eyes through the dancing heat waves. He was apprehensive, ill at ease. Those silent hills ahead were ominous. The air seemed heavy with menace.

'Mebbe it's jest a storm comin' that makes me feel this way,' he muttered.

In the distance loomed the somber portals of Shadow Canyon, through which the trail passed. Between the gorge and the hill top from which Walt glimpsed it was a vast hollow, heavily wooded.

On the very crest of the hill Walt suddenly reined in his horse. Amid the rocks which jumbled the low walls of the canyon something had flashed in the sun. It might be only a bit of mica or a shining flint; but, as Walt told himself:

'Mica flakes and flints don't hop around like they was alive. Nope, that was sunlight glintin' on a rifle barrel or I'm a sheep herder!'

The herd streamed over the hill top and down into the shadow of the trees. Walt called his riders to him.

'Bob, you and Chuck push the dogies right along to the canyon mouth, jest like everythin' was all right,' he ordered two of the punchers. 'But keep yore eyes peeled and be ready to duck for cover. The rest of you leather grabbers come with me.'

He led them in a wide detour to the left, closing in on the canyon slopes more swiftly than the slowly moving herd could approach its mouth. In a dense thicket of manzanita he bade them dismount and tether their horses. 'Bring the rifles,' he directed.

'Oh, my gosh! walkin'!' groaned Hassayampa. 'I'll have blisters till I'll hafta hoof it on my hands.'

'If you make a racket and let Felton's terantulers get the drop on you, yore gonna have blisters on yore face from a jigger pattin' it with a spade,' Walt warned him. 'Let's go, now, they're half-way up the hill, back of them red rocks what overlook the trail.'

Silently the cowboys stole up the slope, flitting ghostlike from rock to rock and tree to tree. They took their time and kept together.

56

From time to time they could catch a glimpse of the reddish boulders behind which Walt had seen the glinting rifle barrel.

Walt, who was well in the lead, halted abruptly, snugged behind a low hedge and motioned his men to come forward stealthily. With the greatest caution they crept up the slope and peered over the ledge.

Crouched back of the red boulders were ten men—long-haired men who held rifles in their hands. In their pose was a terrible expectancy.

Benchleg Bowles cast a questioning glance at Walt. The tall puncher shook his head.

'Wait!' the gesture said plainly as words.

Silence continued. The long-haired drygulchers did not move. Their attention was centered on something invisible to Walt and his men. Abruptly one of them shifted. A shot rang out. Felton's killers leaped to their feet, rifle barrels jutting down toward the Tonto Trail.

'Now!'

Walt's staccato command was echoed by a roar of gunfire. Men went down sprawling beside the red boulders. Others whirled with yells of terror.

Again the Lazy-B rifles flamed. The ground behind the red boulders was a shambles; and still the cold-eyed cowboys poured their fire into the howling group.

Felton's men broke, running like scared rabbits.

57

'Don't let any of 'em get away!' howled Benchleg Bowles, kneeling and firing with care.

As the last of the drygulchers went down, Walt Lee ran forward, a heavy Colt in his hand. He was looking for a face he had not seen.

From a thicket slightly to the left and farther up the slope sounded a clicking of hoofs. Walt swore furiously and raced in that direction.

'The damn sneakin' sidewinder! Kept in clear as usual!' he panted.

CHAPTER EIGHT

VENGEANCE TRAIL

In the thicket tethered horses champed and snorted. Walt jerked a wild-eyed roan free and swung into the saddle. The vicious animal bucked and reared; but the thighs clasping his sides were like bands of spring steel. A grip of iron jerked his head up. Spurs rowelled his flanks. Snorting with rage and pain he shot out of the thicket and down the slope.

Felton had a start, but Walt Lee had the better horse. Slowly but steadily the distance between fugitive and pursuer closed. Felton twisted in the saddle and flung shot after shot at the cowboy. Walt grimly held his fire.

On and on thundered Felton's tall black, his glossy hide flecked white with sweat, his heaving flanks streaming blood. Felton was swiftly killing him.

But the red-eyed roan Walt Lee bestrode had no need of spur or quirt. Vicious, rebellious, intolerant of all restraint, his heart swelled with hate for that black phantom fleeing before him. He slugged his ugly head above the bit, stretched his long legs and fairly poured himself over the ground.

Walt Lee's eyes took on a cold glitter, like jagged ice fanging pale moonlight. He loosened the heavy Colt in his right holster— that gun of vengeance, which bore the initials, 'T. L.' He urged the roan on with voice and hand.

Far ahead shimmered twin ribbons of steel—the C. & P. railroad coiling its way across The Enchanted Mesa toward distant Concha. Up the grade a long material train was climbing. The trail crossed those glistening ribbons in front of the train.

Walt stole anxious glances in the direction of the train as he slowly gained on Felton. He had a queer feeling that the giant engine was racing to beat him to the crossing. If it beat Felton there, that was all right; but if the fugitive dashed across the tracks in front of the engine and Walt was blocked by the following cars, Felton would have an excellent chance to escape. For the first time since the initial round in the thicket, Walt used his spurs on the roan.

The result was not what he had anticipated. Instead of showing greater speed, the roan broke his stride, floundered and pitched. By the time Walt had him in hand again, Felton had gained many precious yards.

Felton was nearing the crossing, making it almost a dead heat with the roaring engine. Walt Lee was hopelessly far behind.

'He's gonna do it, sho' as hell!' muttered the cowboy between stiffening lips. 'Now if this don't beat—'

Suddenly the gods of chance were kind. The black horse stumbled, floundered, staggered almost to a stop and dropped. Felton flung himself free and rolled over and over in the dust. He came to his feet with a rush, eyes glaring wildly. Then he turned and ran madly toward the crossing.

Just before he reached it the engine crashed past, black smoke pouring from her stack, her drivers turning over slowly as she neared the crest of the rise.

Felton rushed on, reached the crossing and ran beside the train. He clutched at the slowly moving cars, gripped a grabiron and was swung off his feet. For a moment he dangled, kicking and clawing; then he got a foot in the stirrup and swarmed up the ladder. From the car top he looked back to where Walt panted up the trail and waved his hand in derision. The laboring engine had dipped over the crest; the wheels were beginning to spin more swiftly.

Walt pulled the roan up, plunging and snorting, his ugly nose flinging back from the rumbling cars that were hurtling past. Walt cast a despairing glance at them.

'I'd jest be stood on my ear if I tried to grab that thing now,' he groaned. 'I can't run half fast enough.'

Suddenly an idea struck him—there was a chance, a desperate chance fraught with danger, but a chance. He whirled the roan and raced him along parallel with the train.

The horse floundered and stumbled over the uncertain footing, snorting his protests. Walt guided him nearer and nearer to the rocking cars.

Shifting the reins from hand to hand, the cowboy loosened his left foot in the stirrup and swung the leg over the horse's neck. For a breathless instant he stood poised on his right foot. Then he dropped the reins and leaped straight for the speeding train.

He crashed against the car side with stunning force, felt himself rushing down toward the grinding wheels. His hand closed on a grabiron with a jerk that almost wrenched his arm from its socket. He floundered, swayed, got a hold with the other hand and climbed the ladder, blood streaming down his face, his head reeling.

He reached the car top and sprawled on it, panting for breath. Something knocked a shower of splinters into his face and he looked up.

A dozen cars ahead, Felton was kneeling, firing carefully. A bullet droned past Walt's ear. Another one clipped a lock of dark hair from his head as he staggered to his feet.

Reeling and weaving, he stumbled across the lurching car tops. Felton continued to fire, retreating slowly as he did so. Walt followed him, shaking the blood from his eyes, gripping Ted Lewis' gun in his sweaty hand.

Felton leaped across the space between two cars and halted, stuffing shells into his empty Colt. Walt ran forward a few more steps, flung his six up and pulled the trigger.

Palely golden in the sunlight, long lances of flame gushed from the black muzzle. Little curls of blue smoke leaped and gamboled fantastically. Felton stopped loading to answer the shots.

'Three—four—five—' Walt counted his bullets. He steadied, swept the blood from his eyes and took deliberate aim.

One instant Felton's eyes were glinting along his gun barrel. The next they were wild with a terrible blank surprise. The killer stiffened, rose on his toes and pitched forward between the cars. The roaring wheels drowned his despairing yell.

The wheels roared on, but the shining surface of some of them was smudged by horrible dark stains!

Walt Lee gazed at Little Ted Lewis' Colt, empty in his hand. Then as the train rumbled over a bridge, he flung the gun far into the deep waters of Crazy Horse river. Its work of vengeance was done!

The Lazy-B rannies brought the trail herd into Concha. Walt Lee met them and led them to Barrington's office. The giant super chuckled gleefully as Walt regaled him with the account of the passing of Felton and his gang. He paid Walt for the cattle in newly minted gold pieces.

'Thought you musta been eatin' *loco* weed when I heard 'bout you maverickin' off to that stampede,' he growled. 'If you ever take a notion yore tired of ranchin', drop around and see me 'fore you take up anythin' else. The road can use men like you.'

Walt grinned and shook his head. 'Guess I got saddle leather and hoss flesh and grass ropes sorta mixed up in my blood,' he said.

He turned to his waddies and counted gold pieces into their surprised hands.

'Jest a little bonus the Old Man told me to give you work dodgers, if we got the herd in,' he explained.

Rawhidin' Dave Barrington dropped a clinking sack on the table.

'And heah's another little one from the

63

railroad,' he rumbled. 'Enj'y yoreselves, boys!'

Hassayampa Hawkins let out a long yell:

'Hi-yi-yi! I'm a bad he-wolf from Bitter Creek and it's my night to howl!'

Outside, Concha's roar was rising to the stars. Music blared, bottles clicked, cards rustled and wheels hummed. From the open doors of the dance-halls came the shuffle of feet and the laughter of women. Walt turned to his fellow punchers and grinned widely.

'C'mon, you jugheads! I craves excitement!'

Down the crowded, color splashed street they bowlegged, wide hats tilted rakishly, spurs jingling, holsters tapping against muscular thighs. Money that ached to be spent chinked musically in their pockets. Lusty life ran riot in their veins. Somebody was bellowing a song:

'The days of old! The days of gold!
The days of Forty-nine!'

A week later Walt Lee again stood before the desk in Captain Tom McDonough's Ranger headquarters. The old fireater had listened to the cowboy's story with many a snort and chuckle. His frosty eyes twinkled as he reached into his desk drawer.

'Come here, you young hellion,' he grunted, 'and bend over, yore too damn tall to reach up to.'

His gnarled old fingers worked for a moment. 'All right,' he said.

64

Walt Lee stood up, smiling proudly. On his left breast gleamed the silver star of the Rangers.

'Here's yore 'pintment,' growled Captain Tom, handing him a folded paper. 'Now let's see what you really got in you!'

Outside the office, Ranger Walt Lee started north and east toward the gray desert that flanked the weird Tonto Hills. Was it chance that drew his gaze in that direction, or was it a vague premonition of what the years held in store for him? For even at that moment a drama was unfolding there in the shadow of the fantastic hills, the first act of a drama in which the Ranger would play a leading role, through which he would walk with death ever at his elbow and sinister mystery as his boon companion.

CHAPTER NINE

THE SECRET OF THE SANDS

The desert was a blue mystery embroidered with star-threads of silver and a-crawl with little golden voices as the sand grains moved one against another. Walking the wings of the wind, those amber grains caressed lonely butte and hillside and canyon wall with fairy finger whose touch was light as thistledown but persistent as the onward march of time.

They were chisel and hammer of the Master Sculptor and their handiwork was the frosted breath of the Eternal Imagination upon the transient windowpane of the ages. Beautiful, awesome, grotesque—the shapes the everlasting stone assumed under their persistent chipping and scouring loomed weirdly in the star gleam and lured or repelled, soothed or menaced. Silent, motionless in the golden flood of the Texas sunshine, they took unto themselves motion and voice when the robe of the night swathed the mighty shoulders of the western mountains and the lonely plaint of the coyote shivered the blue-silver web of the stillness into a myriad haunted fragments of protesting sound.

The man who reeled and staggered across the desert talked to the shadowy sculptures— talked as to old friends and ancient enemies. At times he laughed wildly and the brooding brutes flung back a hollow echo of his mirth. Now and again he fell to his hands and knees and crawled; and then the whispering voices of the shifting sands spoke to him, softly, insistingly, an insidious pleading in their tones.

He cursed the Voices, cursed them feebly, querulously, and staggered to his feet again to escape them.

'You ain't gonna get it!' he raved, slobbering thick words over his swollen black and protruding tongue. 'You ain't gonna get it, damn you! It's mine, you lousy, sneakin' killers! You ain't gonna get it back! I found it! I worked for it! I starved for it! Damn you, I *died* for it!'

His voice rose in a screaming shriek and cracked horribly on a quivering high note—

'It's mine! It's mine! It's mine! You ain't gonna take it back! Damn you! Damn you! Damn you.'

He fell, groaning and retching, lay for long moments, while the sands whispered around him. Then again he staggered to his feet and went reeling through the bleak immensities.

Ahead, far away, glowed a new star, a reddish, wavering star that appeared to swim low above the darkling earth. Too low! The onward whirl of the hurrying world would inevitably dash it in flaming fragments against the wall of the western mountains. The delirious man realized this. He muttered and mumbled about it, dim wonder in his foggy mind that such a gigantic cosmic mistake should have been made. Hazily he resolved to go and see about it. Perhaps it was not too late to rectify this droll but ominous error of Omnipotence. On he staggered, more and more firmly resolved to play the part of a stellar 'Destiny.' And the imperiled star, as if to do its part, did not shoot off into unreachable celestial realms; instead, it waited for him.

The desert wanderer saw this, and exulted

accordingly. On he lurched toward that wavering pinpoint of ruddy light that grew and broadened and at length crackled invitingly. The lost man quickened his wavering steps, chewing words in his gummy mouth. Suddenly he uttered a hoarse, unbelieving cry.

The 'star' was not a star bound to earth by some whim of Creation! It was nothing but a cheerfully burning campfire, in the light of which two men moved about. They heard that gasping cry, froze in uncertain attitudes and peered into the shadows.

Out of those shadows staggered a tattered scarecrow with long, unkempt hair, wild eyes and a burned and battered face. Its tongue, black as old leather, protruded from the writhen lips. Incoherent words dribbled from the gaping mouth and, as if the last savings of strength needed for this supreme effort were exhausted, the starved frame seemed to sink in upon itself and crumble. Even as the younger of the two men leaped forward, it pitched silent and motionless upon the sands.

Followed minutes of efficient activity. They turned the wanderer over, bathed his face with water and wiped his caked lips.

'His pockets are full of rocks or something,' grunted the younger man. 'Get 'em out, Pete, so he can lie easy.'

The older man obeyed, pulling crumbling lumps of stone from the sagging pockets. He pitched them aside, pawed out some more and was about to send them after the first lot. In the act of throwing, his hand froze in midair and he stared with bulging eyes at its contents. Muttering in his beard, he shuffled nearer the fire and peered more closely at the crumbling fragments. He spoke, his voice hoarse and choked—

'Mike, look here!'

The younger man glanced up impatiently. 'What you want?' he demanded. 'This fellow needs attention.'

'So does this—look!'

Grumbling, the younger man leaned toward the fire. Then he too stared with wide eyes and hanging jaw.

The rock appeared to be a sort of spongy cement shot through with lumps of dull yellow. The young man took the fragment, rubbed it, peered at it from all angles.

'Pete, it's gold, sure as you're a foot high!' he marveled. 'Did you ever see anything like it?'

'Never in all my bawn days,' declared the other. 'Them's lumps of gold in there, and they're thick as raisins in a slice of fruit cake. Man wouldn't need to work a croppin' like that for more'n a week to get rich.'

'You figure there's actually a vein of that richness?'

The older man shook his head. 'Not likely,' he said. 'These chunks are more liable to be a freak outcroppin' like the one Whitman was allus lookin' for in Califor'ny and Nevada back in the sixties; but you can lay to it there's mighty val-ble ledge where this came from. Is there any more in his pockets?'

The question brought the young man out of his trance. 'Wait, we've got to see what we can do for this fellow first,' he exclaimed. 'Hand me that water, again.'

Grunting something unintelligible, the other obeyed, but there was a hot glow in his eyes and his sinewy fingers tightened over the fragments of gold-shot rock.

Nevertheless he assisted his companion with the wanderer, who was undoubtedly a very sick man. They forced a few drops of water down his throat and followed it with a trickle of warm soup. Only the first trickle went down, however. The patient either could not or would not swallow. The young man's face became anxious as the labored breathing grew slower and slower.

'I'm afraid he isn't going to make it,' he admitted reluctantly at last. His companion nodded.

''Fraid so, too. Sorta rattlin' in his throat now—that sounds bad. Stopped breathin', ain't he?'

To all appearances he had. The young man could detect no faintest exhalation from the sagging lips. He felt of the shrunken chest, fumbling here and there inside the ragged shirt.

'Can't feel a thing,' he muttered, laying his

70

ear against the emaciated ribs. 'Can't hear anything either,' he added a moment later. 'Guess he's gone, poor devil. Wonder who he is?'

'Look in his pockets,' suggested the other, bending close.

The young man followed the suggestion and turned out a nondescript assortment of odds and ends of scant value. Finally, from an inner pocket, he drew forth a smeary bit of folded paper and what felt like a square of cardboard in a buckskin covering. His companion pounced on the paper and unfolded it. His eyes gleamed as he peered at the orderly arrangement of lines and markings.

'Jest as I callated,' he exulted. 'Mike, this is a map of this feller's diggin's. Here's a location notice, too, all writ out and ready for filin'. Follerin' his back trail with this'll be a pipe! What's that yuh got?'

The young man had undone the buckskin coverings and revealed a small photograph of a dark-eyed girl with a wealth of dark curls clustered above a low, broad forehead. She had a sweet mouth and appeared to be fifteen or sixteen years old. Across the face of the picture was written, 'To Dad, from Betty.'

'His daughter,' murmured the young man pityingly. 'Hello, here's her name and address on the back—"Elizabeth Weston, Lazy-W ranch, Postoffice, Willard."'

'Willard!' repeated the older man. 'Say, let's

71

see that map again.'

He peered at the smeary paper, muttering to himself and tracing the lines with a long finger that trembled slightly.

'Mike,' he exclaimed at length, 'this feller musta got hisself hurt or somethin' 'fore the desert got him. I betcha you me he was headin' for Willard, or tryin' to. He musta been all mixed up and travelin' in circles. Where he's— got his claim marked ain't twenty miles from Willard—that's a ganglin' cow-town, the county seat nigh onto forty miles southeast of here. He jest nacherly headed plumb in the wrong d'rection, that's what he did. Yeah, I betcha a new goot he got hurt.'

The other was already examining the still form by the fire.

'You're right,' he replied gravely. 'Here's a bad cut on his head, just healing; still swollen, too. Wouldn't be surprised if he had a skull fracture. No wonder he got lost, poor devil!'

'What we gonna do 'bout it, Mike?'

'Isn't anything much we can do—for him. Let's lay him over there away from the fire, where we can't see him. He isn't very pleasant to look at. In the morning we'll bury him and then we'll head for Willard and file the location for his daughter and then try and find her. That's the best we can do.'

The older man blinked, and swallowed. For a moment he seemed unable to find the words he desired to speak. When he did speak it was in a strained, choked voice.

'That's—that's liable to be a mighty rich claim.'

'Uh-huh, that's the way I figure it, Pete. Looks like everybody but us has the luck. Not that this fellow was particularly lucky—he found gold, all right, but he also found—a grave. Ever notion, Pete, how the two often go together? I've felt, sometimes, that if I ever do get to handle real rich ore I'll find a grave, too. Ever feel that way?'

Absently he picked up one of the crumbly fragments of rich float and fingered it, while the other mumbled in his gray-streaked beard and stared at the little heap of rich ore with eyes that glowed.

The young man spoke again: 'There's a chance we may be able to stake some good ground ourselves; may be more than one vein where this came from. There are ledges in these hills, lots of them. Perhaps this will be the chance we've been looking for.'

He laid the ore down and picked up the small photograph. 'Pretty girl,' he mused. 'Looks a little like one I used to know back east; younger, though, and got bigger eyes. Sorry we'll be taking her bad news. How we going to carry this ore, in one of the packs?'

'Oughtn't to carry val'ble stuff like that in the packs,' objected the other. 'Packs is allus opened come time to make camp. Sometimes there's strangers 'round at campin' time; they hadn't oughta see it. S'pose you wrap it up and put it in the pocket of that big coat of yores. Be safe there, and out of sight.'

'Good idea,' admitted the young man. 'I'll wrap it up in a piece of that gunnysack.'

A little later he stowed the packet of ore, the picture and the map in a capacious pocket of the heavy coat he often slept in on cool nights. He slipped the coat on now, with a glance at the overcast sky. To the west was a faint rumble of thunder and a wan flicker of distant lightning.

'Going to rain,' he predicted. 'I'll bank the fire good and scoop out a trench around it. Maybe it'll hold then, if it don't pour too hard.'

The other grunted agreement and the two made ready for the night. Half an hour later the young man was sleeping soundly beside the dully glowing fire, his coat wrapped around him. Nearby two shaggy burros grunted contentedly. Overhead the lightning flicker had crept well up the sky; the thunder mutter had become an ominous growl. The air was tense with impending events.

The older man was not asleep, although he lay quietly enough except for the opening and closing of the fingers of one powerful hand. In that hand was a fragment of the rich quartz, which he had, unbeknownst to his companion, pilfered from the wanderer's hoard. His palm was moist and hot over the stone, and there was sweat on his face despite the coolness of

74

the night, and a red glow in his eyes. From time to time he shot speculating glances at his sleeping companion. Overhead the storm gathered in strength.

And in the heart of the bearded man a resolve strengthened. What had been a nebulous thing born of vague impulse was fast becoming a definite driving force that swept all before it. The man muttered words between his clenched teeth, words of justification. His hands opened and closed. One slid to the gun in his belt, clamped the cool butt, dropped away as from something venomous; a shudder convulsed his big frame; but a moment later his hand again slid to the gun's checkered grip.

In the black sky the lightning flared; thunder rumpled hoarsely. The sleeping man stirred, snuggled closer in the folds of his coat and lay still once more.

Slowly, carefully, the bearded man got out of his blankets, his eyes never leaving the sleeping form dimly seen in the glow of the fire. For a moment he paused on his knees; then he rose to his feet with cat-like sureness and glided toward where two packs lay under the slight overhang of a rock. He groped about for a little, turned and gazed long and earnestly across the glowing fire. Then with cautious, purposeful step he glided toward the sleeping man. With the same stealthy caution he dropped to his knees beside him, hands outstretched, gripped weapon poised. Taut whispers breathed through his clenched teeth—

'He ain't got no sense—never will have—stretch out a hand and get rich—wouldn't do it—ain't honest—honest, hell!—ain't nobody honest—fightin' this damn desert more years'n he's lived—chance at last—ain't gonna pass it up!'

The lightning flared again, a lovely blooming of the roses of the storm with petals of flaming gold and a web of fiery foliage. The thunder pealed like the clarion call of a Last Day—*'Vengeance is mine . . .'*

The desert wanderer was not dead, although the faint into which he sank was so deep and cold and so shook the very citadel of his life that it was small wonder that it had caused the two prospectors to believe he had actually cashed in his chips. Now, revived by the cool mist-breath of rain that rode down on the blue wings of the wind, he raised his gaunt form on an elbow and stared about him, his mind for the moment clear, his faculties alert. His gaze centered on the figure crouching in the glow of the fire. For an instant he did not understand; then his eyes darkened with utter horror and a cry rushed to his cracked lips.

Cr-r-rash!

The black vault of the sky seemed to split asunder and dissolve in fragments of liquid frame. The very mountains rocked to the roar of the thunder blast. It wiped the cry from the

76

wanderer's lips as a cloth wipes mist from a window pane. Likewise it drowned the death cry of the sleeping man, if he uttered one. His body convulsed under the blankets, quivered and was still. The wanderer dropped back to the sands, the senses shocked out of him again. Rigid as in death, he lay while the level lances of the rain lashed the earth and a bellowing wind lifted the wet sands in stinging sheets.

The bearded man, weapon poised, glanced up as the lightning blazed. The forked flash seemed to bring inspiration. For a moment, he worked over the head of his victim, arranging the thick hair to cover the wound just above the left temple. Swinging to the fire he raked a glowing brand from beneath the protecting covering that still resisted the rain. Shielding the brand in his cupped hands, he again bent over his victim. With steady fingers he drew the brand down the side of the dead face, searing the flesh jaggedly. With a croaking chuckle he tossed the brand aside.

'Lightnin' hits in all sorts of funny places,' he mumbled. 'If anybody finds him 'fore the coyotes does, chances are they'll think jest that. Now to get goin'.'

Swiftly he plucked the map, the parcel of gold ore and the picture from the dead man's pockets. The picture he thrust into the still glowing heart of the fire. The ore and the map he carefully stowed away. In a trice he had one of the burros loaded with a ready pack. With

77

the rain and the wind lashing out his trail as swiftly as he made it, he forged away from the camp, heading south by east. Behind him, around him, with him, the sands hissed and whispered. He cowered away from the Voices and the wet leer of the sinister buttes.

The wanderer again recovered from his swoon as dawn was graying the sky. The rain was still falling and the wind shifting the sands. Dizzily he got to his feet, his eyes blank, words drolling over his cracked lips. He glanced about him with insane cunning, shrank away from the drenched corpse, peered at the patient burro huddled over the overhand of the rock.

There was food in a covered skillet beside the craftily banked fire, the remains of the prospectors' evening meal, and a pot half filled with coffee. Beneath its bank the fire still glowed.

The man ate of the food, his strength returning with each voracious mouthful. He rooted the coffee pot into the heart of the glowing coals until it boiled. The hot liquid revived him still more. Just as the watery ghost of the drowned dawn struggled up the long ladder of the eastern sky he loaded the burro and once more plunged into the desert. Behind him the dead man lay stark in his reeking blanket.

Tom Webb and Lapp Hanson of the K Bar L, cutting across the desert to Willard, found the corpse. Dismounting, they squatted beside it. Webb pointed to the seared cheek.

'Lightnin'! what yuh know 'bout that!' he exclaimed. 'Killed him while he was sleepin'!'

'Liable to hit most anywhere,' agreed Lapp, 'and last night was a lulu. Say, wonder where this jigger's outfit is? Ain't nothin' in sight but this blanket he's sleepin' in. Fire for cookin', but nothin' to cook with.'

'Mebbe he had a hoss or a burro and it bolted with his pack durin' the storm,' hazarded Webb.

'Folks don't load a hoss or a burro and leave it standin' loaded all night,' grunted Lapp disdainfully. 'Nope, that ain't the answer. Pore feller, ain't much more'n a kid. Prospector, I reckon. Woods is full of 'em.'

A lock of wet hair straggled over one of the staring eyes. Lapp automatically brushed it back. Then his lanky frame tensed, his lean jaw tightened and he stared at what his hand had uncovered.

'Look here, Tom,' he snapped.

Webb, who had been looking over the camp, turned quickly and followed his bunky's silently pointing finger. Just above the dead man's left temple, where the hair began to grow, was a small round hole.

'Shot!' grunted Webb. 'Shot shore as hell!'

'Small calibre gun, too,' said Lapp, eyeing the hole expertly. 'Wonder if the slug come out.'

He gently turned the body over and examined the head. 'Nope, she stayed in,' he nodded. 'Well, what d'yuh know 'bout this!'

Webb shook his head. 'Too much for me,' he declared. 'Callate we'd better notify the sheriff.'

The sheriff, who was also the coroner, rode up from Willard, looked the body over and also shook his head. The only thing he could discover was a name printed on a rectangle of cloth sewed on the inside of the dead man's heavy coat. 'Michael Hubbell,' read the name. There had once been an address, but it had long since faded out.

'Now who the hell's Michael Hubbell?' demanded the sheriff. Nobody could tell him.

The sheriff buried the body beside the rock where it lay and smeared the name on the huge boulder that acted as headstone. He took the coat to his office along with the few trifles the dead man's pockets contained, put it away and forgot all about it.

CHAPTER TEN

A RANGER DIES

A welter of sweating activity, Laska sprawled in the lap of a purple-blue mountain whose lofty head looked across the Rio Grande and far into Mexico. The dust of her unpaved streets danced to the constant thunder of stamp mills and trembled when, deep in the earth beneath, a faint jar and rumble told of blasts set off in the long galleries of the Monarch mine or those of the lesser diggings that had given the turbulent town birth a few years previous.

Laska was a boiling hive of industry under the hot Texas sun. She was an equally boiling sink of iniquity under the silver blaze of the Texas stars. To her saloons, dancehalls, gambling halls and pleasure palaces came cowboys from the big ranches to the north and east, prospectors from the hills, Mexicans from the river towns. Here also came a more sinister element to mingle with the blue-shirted miners and the lean plainsmen. Smugglers from below the Line were wont to pass that way, using the Sanlucar Trail through nearby Black Rock Canyon. They stopped off at Laska for news and diversion. Bandits, and gentlemen who had engagements with sheriffs which they had no desire to keep, also used the Sanlucar Trail or others even more devious and sinister which slip-wriggled through the Tonto Hills. They too found Laska a place of singular charm.

The general result was a hell-brew that would have poisoned the sidewinders of the desert had they not the good sense to keep away from Laska and all of her doings. Laska boiled under the sun and bellowed under the stars. There were no keys to the saloon doors and the undertaker's shop was the busiest place in town. When a Laska citizen actually died a natural death the occurrence was celebrated as a notable event and the mines granted a holiday!

Ten miles to the northeast was Willard, the county seat, little more than a hamlet. To the south and west was the hot shimmer of the desert with its badland jumble of fantastically curved buttes and its whispering sands. To the east and south the Tonto Hills flung their weirdly colored spires into the blue of the sky. Between Laska and Willard began the rolling rangeland broken by hill and mesa and slashed by grass-grown canyons through which white water foamed.

Five men rode up to the Laska bank, which was situated on a quiet side street. With businesslike efficiency they shot the cashier through the head, split the president's scalp with a gun barrel and rode away with a fifty-thousand-dollar mine payroll. A posse was hastily formed and a messenger dispatched hotfoot to the sheriff at Willard. Another went to look for Curt Gordon, the Texas Ranger assigned to the turbulent mining town. The posse rode hotfoot on the trail of the bandits, having but a vague idea where that trail led or in what direction.

Ranger Gordon did not ride with the posse. Curt Gordon was a young man with ideas of his own. By diligent and persistent questioning he wormed an important piece of information from the still hysterical bank clerk.

'I don't think I would recognize any of them—they were all masked,' the youth admitted, 'but I would know the horse one of them rode if I ever saw it again. It was a sort of brown horse with a white face and half of one of its ears had been cut or shot away. I saw it plain as they rode off.'

Curt Gordon was greatly pleased. He had a theory and proceeded to put it to the test.

'I got a plumb good notion what them hellions will do,' he told himself as he left the bank. 'They ain't gonna hide out in the hills like ev'body thinks. Why should they? The hills ain't safe for nobody with that much money on 'em, and Mexico is jest as bad. They was masked and nobody saw their faces. Where would they be sittin' purtier than right here in Laska? Gents with plenty of money to spend is plumb common hereabouts and don't 'tract no attention. Them jiggers will jest scoot 'round through the hills, lose that fool posse 'thout no trouble and sneak back inter town one at a time when it comes dark. Folks is ridin' in and out all the time and nobody would notice 'em. I betcha a purty I'm right.'

Whereupon Curt Gordon ate a hearty meal, had a smoke and a drink and repaired to his room to rest and wait for the dark. He even slept a while against the possibility of being up all night. It was well after dark when he left his room and sauntered up the busy main street.

There were several livery stables in town and a hitchrack in front of nearly every saloon. Curt first gave his attention to the hitchracks. Later he visited the stables. Then back to the hitchracks. It was close to midnight before he found what he was seeking. Hitched in front of a rattletrap little saloon on the western outskirts of the town was a blaze-faced roan with a mutilated ear. Curt Gordon crouched in the shadows across the street and waited for the owner of the roan to appear.

'Chances are he jest stopped there for a drink,' the Ranger reasoned. 'If he did, he'll be out soon and headin' for the gen'ral meetin' place. If this is it, the rest of the gang'll hive up in there as they drift in. Anyhow, he's gotta come out sometime.'

The rider of the roan, a gangling, stoop-shouldered individual of swarthy complexion, appeared shortly, wiping his moustache with a horny hand. He swung into the saddle and rode slowly down the street. After him glided Curt Gordon. The rider dismounted in front of the El Dorado saloon, tied his horse and entered.

The El Dorado was a big place run by one Bull Barty. Among other things it boasted several 'back rooms' where private parties could be held by gentlemen desiring to avoid the limelight. Well heeled ranchers and mine owners and officials often used those rooms for quiet games of poker. Curt suspected that the rooms had other uses less innocent. He passed through the swinging doors directly behind the rider of the roan, who paid no attention to him in the crowd. He watched the man speak with a bartender, apparently asking a question. The bar-keep jerked a thumb toward a closed door. The man knocked on this and passed through.

Curt Gordon knew the El Dorado. He knew that the room the man had entered could be reached by means of a hallway and a side door into the building. He sauntered carelessly out the swinging doors, turned a corner and dodged into an alley. He found the side door unlocked and glided into the passage. It was dimly lighted by a small bracket lamp. Curt located the closed door of the room he sought without difficulty. Pressing his ear to the panels he listened. He could hear a rumble of voices inside the room but could not make out what was said. Then he heard the muffled sound of an opening and closing door and immediately afterward a voice spoke clearly.

'Here's Whitey—that makes all five. Now—'
The voice trailed off in a jumble of sound. Curt Gordon smiled thinly and loosened his heavy guns in their holsters. Slowly, gently, careful not to make the slightest sound, he turned the doornob, felt the tumbler ease back and the door swing slightly on its hinges; it was

not locked. He hurled it wide open and stepped into the room, a gun in each hand.

Four men were seated at a round table; the fifth was in the act of pulling up a chair. Curt's voice blared at them—

'Elevate!'

There was death in the Ranger's voice and the quintet, 'caught settin',' hastened to obey. Frozen in strained attitudes by his utterly unexpected appearance, they shot their hands into the air and were motionless, glaring at him with hate-filled eyes.

They were a hard-bitten lot and different from the general run of bandits. Courage was stamped on their faces, and intelligence. Even now Curt could see that brains were working at hair-trigger speed, seeking some way out of the situation. He knew that these men had too much sense to go for weapons under the menace of his rock-steady guns; but he knew also that they would not miss a trick. The slightest false move on his part would instantly be taken advantage of. For a split second he studied his captives, his own mind working swiftly. Before they could recover from the first paralysis of astonishment he acted.

'On yore feet!' he bit at the seated four. 'All right, 'bout face, all of you! That's it, faces to the wall. Now, you on the left, bring yore hands down slow—*damn slow*—pull yore hardware and drop it on the floor. One funny move and yuh're so fulla holes nobody'll be able to see you for the light shinin' through! All right, get yore hands up again. Now the next man—take it easy—slow!'

Pair after pair of heavy guns clattered on the floor. The bandits hissed curses through set teeth, but they obeyed. There were no cowards among them, but resisting a Ranger at any time was bad business, and a Ranger with the drop on them was altogether too much. The last gun thumped on the boards and Curt relaxed a trifle. Then he stiffened again and stood with one eye slanted over his shoulder, tensely alert. Steps were sounding in the corridor by which he had entered, coming toward the room. Curt's left-hand gun swung around a trifle to cover the opening. His finger tightened on the trigger. The newcomer stepped into the room, blinking at the tableau it presented. Curt Gordon sighed deep relief as he recognized the visitor.

'Gosh, this is fine!' he exclaimed. 'Yuh're the last puhson I 'spected to see come through that door. These here gents is them what held up the bank this mawnin'. You jest hold yore gun on 'em while I c'lect them hawglegs on the floor.'

'Shore,' said the new arrival, stepping up behind Curt. The Ranger turned back to the prisoners, lowering his guns.

'I'll get—a-a-ah!'

Blood gushed from the Ranger's mouth and nose, drowning the cry in his throat. He whirled about, guns dropping from his nerveless hands. In a last death struggle he threw himself upon the man who had stabbed him in the back and they crashed to the floor together. A moment later the murderer got to his feet, wiping his long blade on the dead Ranger's coat. He snapped terse orders to the five men who crowded around him—

'Get his body outa here—dump it in the alley where it's dark—be careful nobody sees you—mop up the blood with yore handkerchiefs—don't throw 'em away, put 'em in yore pockets. Then get the cards out and start the game 'fore somebody comes in. Hell, no, it waren't heerd in the saloon; they're makin' so much fuss in there they couldn't hear nothin'. Where's the swag—in that saddlebag? Hold the bag on yore knees under the table, Whitey, and divide 'er up while we pertend to play. All right, get set!'

A few minutes later, when a bartender tapped on the door with a round of drinks, a quiet poker game for big stakes was in progress, at least so far as the barkeep could see.

CHAPTER ELEVEN

THE DARK RIDER

Captain Tom McDonough sat in Ranger headquarters at Franklin, that far western post of the Frontier Legion which was bringing law—Ranger law—west of the Pecos, where for generations men had boasted there was no law. There was a furrow between Captain Tom's shaggy white brows as he listened to the words of the well dressed, gentlemanly stranger of advanced years who sat on the far side of the desk. The man had given his name as 'Henry K. Hubbell' and his address as 'New York City.'

'Yes, the man was undoubtedly my son Michael,' Hubbell was saying. 'The sheriff at Willard showed me his coat—I have it here with me in my suitcase—and I immediately recognized it as one my son bought before leaving home on this wild adventure which brought about his untimely death. When nearly four years passed and I heard no word from him, I started out to look for him. I traced him to this locality—he was last seen in the company of an elderly prospector unknown to my informant. The man, a keeper of a store, was positive that the younger man was my son; he instantly identified the

89

photograph I showed him and recalled being impressed by the expensive outfit my son purchased before striking into the desert. He recalled the incident even after the passage of years.'

'Strikes me you waited a tarnation long time 'fore decidin' to look the kid up,' commented Captain Tom.

The other flushed and his eyes were miserable. 'The fact is, Captain, I had quarreled with my son,' he admitted. 'That was his reason for leaving home. I am a business man, have always been a business man. My son took no interest in business. His was a roving, Bohemian nature. He sought adventure, loved the outdoors. He came here with some wild intention of making a fortune and justifying his course in my sight. I was very angry with him, I am sorry to say, and it took me a long time to realize that, after all, blood is thicker than water and that I would gladly give all I possess to have my son safe again. Now it is too late. All I can hope for is vengeance upon his murderer.'

Captain Tom nodded his white head. 'I recall the case,' he said. 'Sheriff Rice of Willard reported it to me. Rice said the feller was shot in the haid with a small-calibre gun. 'Pears the killer had burned the side of his face to make it look like he was struck by lightnin' durin' the storm the night before. Clumsy bus'ness, too, 'cause he took both outfits 'long with him and left the body where anybody could see it had been deserted. There waren't no clues to the killer and what with the Comanches actin' up and the trouble 'long the border 'bout them, there waren't much time to try and figger out a lone killin'. Purty soon ev'body jest nacherly forgot 'bout it, I reckon.'

'Doubtless,' agreed Hubbell. 'Well, Captain, I am here to cause people to refresh their memories; I intend to offer a suitable inducement. I am a rich man, Captain McDonough. I intend to offer a reward to two hundred thousand dollars for evidence that will lead to the capture and conviction of the person or persons who murdered my son. I am prepared at this moment to place in your hands a certified check for that amount, which you will deposit in a suitable bank, the reward to be laid when in your judgment the proper time has arrived.'

Captain Tom stared at the speaker. His lips pursed in a soundless whistle.

'That's a right smart passel of money,' he commented. 'Well—'

He broke off suddenly and called his clerk from the outer office.

'Walt Lee's gettin' ready to ride, ain't he?' he asked the clerk.

'No, suh,' replied the clerk, 'he's done ready. Waitin' outside to talk to you right now.'

'Send him in,' growled Captain Tom.

91

The clerk vanished with a nod and a moment later the door opened again and a man entered. The newcomer had to turn his shoulders slightly to get them through the opening, although it had been plenty wide for the clerk, a stalwart six-footer. Likewise he had to stoop a little to avoid striking the crown of his broad-brimmed hat. He glanced at Captain Tom inquiringly but said nothing. Henry Hubbell studied him with interest. Even a city business man could appreciate the powerful figure with its mighty sweep of shoulders, its deep chest, its lean, supple waist and hips and long line of limb. Lee's face was deeply bronzed, his mouth was firm and rather wide, his nose straight. He removed his hat and laid it on a chair, revealing a broad, thoughtful forehead and thick, crisp black hair.

But it was the eyes that caught the city man's gaze and held it. They were very long, darkly lashed and of a peculiar shade of gray-green. Henry Hubbell did not know it, but they were the type of eyes the West had long ago learned to associate with death sudden and sharp—the eyes of men who glared through a mist of powder smoke into the muzzles of flaming guns. Most of the killers of the Old West had such eyes. So also had those intrepid peace officers who brought justice and order to a wild and disorderly land and made of it a decent place in which decent folk might live.

'Walt,' said Captain Tom, 'I want you to

92

know Mr. Henry Hubbell of New York. He has a story he wants to tell you.'

Lee extended his hand and smiled, and of a sudden his cold eyes were sunny as the waters of a southern sea and his rugged face became singularly pleasant. He gripped Hubbell's hand with slim, steely fingers, and the city man felt a sudden surge of confidence within himself. He breathed deeply as Lee sat down, and plunged again into his story.

Walt Lee listened gravely, asking a question from time to time. Hubbell finished and glanced at him expectantly.

'What do you say, Mr. Lee?' he asked. 'Will you take the matter in hand?'

Walt Lee slowly shook his head. 'I'm 'fraid I won't have the time, suh,' he replied. 'Right now I'm headin' out on a purty bad lookin' case and by the time that's done the chances are there'll be another waitin' for me—this is a purty turbulent section, you know. You see, I ain't a detective, Mr. Hubbell. I'm a Texas Ranger, and a Ranger can't give all his time to what is a sorta private case.'

'I would be willing to offer an even larger reward,' tempted Hubbell.

Walt smilingly shook his head again. 'It ain't the money what counts, suh,' he explained. 'Shucks,' he added with a whimsical grin, 'what'd I do with all them pesos anyhow? I can't nohow eat that much ham-and-eggs!'

Captain Tom threw in what appeared to be

an utterly irrelevant remark—

'Two hundred thousand dollars would build a heap o' schools for Mexican and Injun kids.'

A glow suddenly birthed in the depths of Lee's strange eyes. A tightening of muscles rippled along his lean jaw.

'It shore would,' he admitted thoughtfully. 'All right, suh,' he nodded to Captain Tom, 'if you're 'greeable, I'll put in all the spare time I got on this bus'ness.'

Henry Hubbell drew a deep breath. 'I feel confident,' he said, his voice unsteady, 'that I shall live to see the murderer of my son brought to justice.'

'P'haps,' nodded Lee, 'can't tell. You say you got that coat with you? I'd sorta like to look at it if you're 'greeable.'

Hubbell produced the coat, dusty and slightly mildewed, and Walt examined it. He went through the pockets with painstaking care but unearthed nothing of value. In one side pocket was a small hole through which the tall Ranger poked a tentative finger. Suddenly his eyes narrowed and he probed deeper with the finger. Inside the lining he could feel something rough. With a quick movement of a powerful hand he ripped the lining and drew forth the object. Three heads bent over it intently; Captain Tom swore softly.

''Pears like yore son mighta hit somethin' party val'ble 'fore he got cashed in,' Walt remarked to Hubbell. 'This is 'bout the richest

94

chunk of gold-bearin' quartz I ever laid eyes on.'

'What—what does it mean?' asked the bewildered Hubbell.

'It means,' Walt told him, 'that we got what's allus needed in a case of this kind—we got the motive. There's allus a reason for a killin', and if you can find out that reason you got somethin' to work on; it's a lot easier to run down a reason than to run down a killer. If your son happened to stumble on a rich ledge—as this hunk of rock sorta says he did— then there was a motive for his partner or somebody to kill him. The killer's next move would be to get the ledge. Ledges don't run away and even after they're worked out they leave a hist'ry behind 'em; and that hist'ry ties up with the hist'ry of the man what worked the ledge. 'Fore we found this rock there waren't hardly any chance of ever runnin' down the feller what killed your son. Now there is a chance, though it may be a mighty slim one.'

He carefully wrapped up the bit of gold ore and placed it in an inner pocket. Then he shook hands with Hubbell, nodded to Captain Tom and sauntered out of the office.

'I thought that little reminder 'bout the schools would get him,' Captain Tom chuckled after the door had closed. 'You see, Walt takes a pow'ful int'rest in Injuns and Mexicans—says they're good citizens in the makin' and what with all the marryin' with whites and sich, the kids what is growin' up now will mean a lot to Texas some day. Walt figgers they'd oughta have a chance and he says ed'cation is important. Walt's a ed'cated man hisself—two years in college studyin' minin' engineerin'. Father lost his ranch 'cause of droughts and blizzards and died. Walt hadda give up school and go to punchin' cows again. Then he got inter the Rangers, two years ago, and now he's Lieutenant of this troop and the ace-man of the Ranger outfit. Old Lieutenant Bayles once said he was death on a yaller hoss, called him the Dark Rider, and he's jest that—a plumb holy terror. Most allus works alone—I never bother him with reg'lar routine bus'ness. He's shore handled some tough assignments and handled 'em plumb satisfactory. Yeah, I'll keep in touch with you, suh, and let you know if anythin' develops. I'll deposit this check right away, and here's hopin' the Dark Rider'll claim it to build schools for his greasers and Injuns with.'

Hubbell left the post headquarters and McDonough called for Walt Lee.

'We'll jest mosey down to the undertakers and you can look over what's left of pore Curt Gordon,' he told the Dark Rider. 'Sheriff Rice sent him in jest as they found him. Rice callated we'd wanta see him the way they picked him up behind that damn saloon.'

A few minutes later they were gazing into the pallid, blood-streaked face of Ranger

Gordon. Walt examined the body with the greatest care. He grunted as he pulled Gordon's heavy guns from their sheaths. Neither had been fired.

'You say Rice was certain nothin' had been touched?' he asked.

'That's what he said,' replied Captain Tom. 'He's jest like they found him.'

Lee frowned at the guns. 'Well,' he said, 'somebody shore had these lawglegs outa their pens after Curt was dead.'

'What makes you say that?' wondered Captain Tom.

'Because,' Walt replied, 'they weren't in the right holsters. This is the gun what fits in the right holster; it was in the left, stuck so tight you couldn't hardly get it out. Curt was one of them fellers what carries dif'rent makes of guns. This is a Colt. T'other is a Smith and Wesson. They ain't built jest the same and they don't fit inter each other's holsters. Curt Gordon wouldn't never have shifted them guns in his hands and put them where they didn't b'long. I callate Curt had them irons in his hands when he was downed. He had them pulled on somebody and somebody else got him from behind. Funny thing—he had ears like a Injun and was almighty quick on the trigger. Almost looks like there was somebody behind him he knew and trusted—somebody what downed him plumb onexpected. Hell, there's dirt in the muzzle of this Smith—

97

choked with it! This iron was dropped on the ground and picked up by somebody what never expected to use it—picked up and jammed inter the wrong sheath.' He carefully knocked the plug of dirt onto the palm of his hand, stared at it a moment and dropped it into a pocket.

Captain Tom shook his white head in admiration. 'Ain't anythin' you miss, is there?' he marveled. 'Now what you found?'

Lee was carefully unwinding something from around the dead man's right coat sleeve button. He held it up for McDonough to see.

'Looks like Curt closed with the jigger and pulled some of his hair out,' he commented.

Captain Tom frowned at the snarled strand. 'Ain't many fellers wear their hair that long,' he remarked. 'Would almost say it was a woman's.'

'Too coarse for a woman's,' Lee disagreed. 'Nope I'll betcha this come off a man's head. Oughtn't to be hard to run down a jigger with hair that length. Of course Gordon mighta picked that up some other way 'fore he was killed, but it's wuth thinkin' 'bout.'

Further examination of the body revealed nothing of value other than that the wound which caused death had undoubtedly been made from behind with a long, thin blade.

'You say Hubbell is gonna leave his son's body where it's buried?' Walt asked as they left the undertaker's shop.

'Uh-huh,' replied Captain Tom. 'He said the kid loved the country and he callates he'd rather sleep there than in some fancy city graveyard. He left money with Sheriff Rice to have a monyment cut and set up. Callate yuh'll be passin' purty close to the place on yore way to Laska. Yeah, I figger it's a good idea not to let anybody over there know that yuh're a Ranger. Well, good luck, Walt.'

As the sun of early afternoon was turning the desert to a sea of gold, Walt Lee rode out of Franklin. To the south was the silvery Rio Grande, to the east, beyond the desert, the madly colored Tonto Hills. All about him were the leering buttes and frowning canyon walls. And as he rode, the sands whispered to him, chuckling evilly, mocking him with their hidden mysteries, defying him to ferret out their grim secrets. Astride his magnificent golden sorrel he rode with the scarlet and gold and mauve and saffron of the sunset at his back and the blue breathlessness of the approaching dusk walking toward him out of the east. Deadly danger awaited him there beyond the star dusted rim of the horizon, danger and treachery and the loathsome offspring of ruthless greed; but the Dark Rider's green eyes were sunny and the corners of his firm mouth quirked as with pleasant anticipation.

CHAPTER TWELVE

YAQUI GUNS

It was a bitter ride across the desert. Walt purposefully set out late in the afternoon in order to escape the heat as much as possible. It was well after dark when he found himself in line with a peculiar butte formation due south of a hill spire that Henry Hubbell had described as marking the lonely grave of his son. Both butte and towering crag were shadowy and unreal in the moonlight, but Walt, with the plainsman's uncanny sense of distance and direction developed to the fullest degree, was confident they were the formations in question. He did not, however, turn aside and ride the three or four miles out of his course necessary to bring him to the site of the grave. After all he was on Ranger business, and that brooked no delay for private enterprises. Besides, he doubted if anything of value was to be discovered in the neighborhood of the grave. Any markings or clues left at the time of the murder would have long since been washed away by the tireless fingers of the eternally drifting sands. Perhaps at some later date, when he had time at his disposal, he would visit young Michael Hubbell's last resting place. Right now his

100

paramount interest was the solving of the brutal murder of Ranger Curt Gordon and the bringing of his killers to justice. That could not wait or be subordinated to any other issue. His lean jaw tightened as he thought on the matter and his green eyes were bleakly cold. There was a price demanded for a Ranger slain, a price that must be paid in full. True to Ranger custom, Walt Lee carried in a shoulder holster, as a supplement to his own heavy Colts that tapped against his muscular thighs, one of Curt Gordon's guns. That gun was a gun of vengeance. Perhaps he would never have to use it. Perhaps the regular process of law would bring the supreme penalty to the murderer. But just the same Curt Gordon's gun rested ready to his hand in case of need.

Walt rode until the golden arrows of the dawn shot up the sky. Then he made camp on the cool shadow of a canyon wall, cooked and ate a simple breakfast and went to sleep. Goldy, the big sorrel, filled his stomach with rich grasses, drank his fill and drowsed contentedly through the hot hours. Dusk found them on the trail once more. Walt wanted to strike Laska in the daytime if possible, so he made camp while the night was still dark and got an early start the following day. He did not ride directly to the mining town but skirted it to the south and rode on toward Willard, the county seat. A little later he would turn back and enter Laska from the northeast, the logical direction from which a wandering cowboy would drift into town. With Ranger thoroughness he would miss no bets; riding in from the southwest might create suspicion in some observing minds, which was the last thing the Dark Rider desired. He struck a pretty well defined trail and followed it. The desert was changing to rangeland and clumps of mesquite and other chapparral were displacing cactus and greasewood. Here and there, groves of cottonwoods or burr oaks provided welcome shade. Waterholes began to make their appearance, and an occasional stream. Walt eyed the country with a cattleman's eye of appreciation.

'Purty darn nice range, looks like,' he concluded. 'Darn sight more lastin' value here than the mines they're makin' such a fuss about. Well—'

He suddenly broke off, his gaze fixed on the distances before him. 'Now who's that in such a hell of a hurry?' he wondered.

It looked like a nervous puffing of smoke where the trail wound toward a clump of low hills, but Walt knew it was in reality a dancing dust cloud kicked up by many swift hoofs. A little later he determined it to be the work of a sizeable herd of cattle.

'What in blazes is the idea of hustlin' a flock of dogies along like that?' he demanded. 'They're runnin' pounds off 'em ev'ry mile. E'vthing considered, this don't look so good.'

In a few minutes the herd materialized beneath the dust cloud as a clump of bouncing dots. He could not as yet make out the riders.

'Callate they don't see me either,' he mused. 'Well, they don't need to, just yet.'

Less than a hundred yards from the trail was a thick clump of mesquite. Walt turned the sorrel aside and rode for the thicket. Goldy wormed his way into it, snorting disgustedly at the thorns. Walt left him in the centre of the clump and glided back to where he could peer through the outer fringe of twigs.

On came the herd, long horns tossing, red eyes rolling. Walt could hear the querulous bawling of the tired dogies as they were hustled along. Now he could make out the riders, and as they drew nearer his lean jaw tightened and he instinctively loosened his heavy guns in their sheaths.

There was no mistaking those sinewy, dark-faced horsemen mounted on shaggy ponies. Hatless, their straight black hair cut in a square bang across the forehead and held in place by a band of bright colored cloth, garbed in fringed buckskin, they sat their flat saddles with the ease and grace of men who had spent their lives on horseback. They carried shortbarreled rifles and each had a knife or hatchet in his belt. Two also boasted heavy sixes.

'Yaquis,' Walt muttered. 'Yaquis from 'crost the river, rustlin' a herd.'

103

Tense, eager, he watched as the herd swept toward him, planning just what to do. He finally decided to let the rustlers pass him and then ride forth while they were still within rifle range. He knew that his own heavy Winchester snugged in the saddle-boot would carry farther than the old-model guns of the Indians. Also their wiry mustangs were no match for the great sorrel either in speed or endurance. The raiders would be forced to either abandon the herd and flee for the river or be picked off one by one by the cool marksman riding in their rear. Walt smiled grimly as the four Yaquis, closely bunched in the rear of the lumbering herd, came directly opposite the thicket. He half turned to where Goldy waited patiently.

But the Dark Rider, wise though he was in the furtive ways of Indians, had underestimated the craftiness of the raiders from below the Line. A fifth Yaqui had ridden far in front and to one side of the laboring herd. He spotted the Ranger and saw him ride into the thicket. Forthwith he had signalled his companions who instantly understood but gave no sign. Only Walt's uncannily swift perception of the even slightly unusual saved him. The close bunching of the raiders warned him that something was amiss. They should have been spread out about the herd. Why weren't they? In the act of turning to his horse he swung back, slim, bronzed hands dropping to the butts of his Colts.

Without the slightest warning the four Yaquis wheeled their mustangs from the trail and charged the thicket. The distance they had to cover was scant and had Walt been in the act of mounting, they would have been all over him before he could fire a shot. As it was, his heavy guns were flaming before the Indians were half way to the thicket. Two went out of the saddles as if swept by a giant hand, drilled dead centre.

But they were fighters, those grim, high-nosed riders from the purple mountains of Mexico. Yelling, shooting, the remaining two hurled their horses straight into the muzzles of the Ranger's flaming guns. A third went down at the very edge of the thicket. The fourth crashed through the growth and left his saddle in a streaking dive, gleaming knife flung high.

Hampered by the close growing mesquite, Walt could not altogether avoid the blood-maddened savage. He pulled trigger a last time and knew he had not missed; but the Yaqui, blood spouting from a flesh wound in his upper arm, struck the Ranger squarely in the chest with a sinewy shoulder. Down they went together, hitting, gouging, clawing.

Walt's right-hand gun was knocked spinning. His other was empty. In the nick of time he caught a corded wrist as the long blade plunged toward his heart. A wrench and a twist and the knife was turned aside. The Yaqui clawed desperately at his face and

105

throat, but was unable to get a killing grip. Walt whirled over sideways and let drive with his right fist. His bunched knuckles, hard as iron, driven with the speed of a rifle bullet, crashed against the Yaqui's jaw. The redman quivered and stiffened out. Walt scrambled to his knees, clawing for his fallen guns. He flung erect

and in the same movement hurled himself headlong. A rifle roared and a bullet yelled through the air where his body had been the instant before. Walt's Colt blazed from where he lay prone on the ground and the fifth Yaqui, who had come worming through the mesquite, pitched forward on his face, blood bubbling from his mouth and the gaping wound in his throat.

Walt got to his feet, stuffing fresh shells into his guns. He listened intently, peering through the mesquite, tense and ready for further attack. There was no sound, however, other than the bleat and mutter of the tired herd which had halted a little distance down the trail and was milling restlessly. Walt holstered his guns and took stock of the situation.

Four of the raiders were dead. The man he had knocked out was still unconscious and had a nasty hole in his arm, from which blood oozed sluggishly. Walt speculated the senseless savage.

'Callate that jigger'll be purty darn sick when he wakes up,' he decided. 'He'll be plumb satisfied to head for home 'thout raisin' any more hell. I don't want to bother with a prisoner jest now and the yarn he'll take back to the rest of the hellions down there oughta help keep 'em away from this section for a spell. Guess I'll best leave that punctured gent where he is. Figger, anyhow, it's up to me to run them dogies back in the direction they come and that'll be plenty chore 'thout havin' a perf-rated buck on my hands. Let's get goin', Goldy hoss, chances are we're a damn long ways from somewhere. Gosh, I feel like I'd been shoved through a knot hole and hung up on a cactus to dry!'

He was bruised and battered but had no injury worthy of concern. The cattle were too tired to offer more than a bawling protest as he turned their noses to the north again. He had nudged the herd along for not more than a couple of miles when once again an ominous dust cloud danced up from the trail ahead.

CHAPTER THIRTEEN

LAW OF THE ROPE

Puckering his eyes against the dazzle of sunlight, the Dark Rider studied the dust cloud. It did not take him long to conclude that it was not cattle this time. A half dozen or so horsemen were riding swiftly along the trail. He loosened his Colts in their sheaths and drew his saddlegun from the sheath and assured himself it was in proper working order. He balanced the rifle in front of him and rode on behind the plodding herd, carelessly at his ease but with every sense alert.

The tight group of riders took individual form as it swept toward the herd. Walt speculated them through narrowed lids.

'Not Injuns this time, anyhow,' he muttered, purposely dropping a bit farther behind his grumbling charges.

The riders skirted the herd and pulled up their horses. The leader raised his hand. Walt rode a little closer and also pulled up. The leader rode forward a few more paces. He was a tall man, lean and sinewy, with a wide spread of shoulders. His face was handsome with its firm mouth, high-bridged nose and cold blue eyes. There was something of menace and authority in the eyes and in the pose of his big body. On his sagging vest twinkled a silver star.

'Looks like I'm up 'gainst the local law,' mused Walt. 'Wonder what kinda deal he's callatin' on dishin' out?'

The sheriff spoke, his voice clear and ringing: 'Who are you, feller? Where you headin' for, and where'd you pick up them steers?'

For a moment Walt did not answer. He was studying the sheriff and the cold-eyed men who rode behind him. He read suspicion on their faces and tense readiness for anything in their pose.

'Well?' prompted the sheriff.

Walt swept him with his level green gaze. 'Betcha me yuh're a lot better at askin' questions than answerin' 'em,' he drawled.

The sheriff's jaw dropped slightly then snapped shut like a spring trap; a flush burned on his high cheek bones and seemed to redden his eyes. His upper lip lifted like that of a snarling dog, revealing white, even teeth.

'That kinda talk won't get you nowhere!' he snarled.

'And askin' questions in the tone o' voice you used won't get you no answers,' Walt told him quietly.

For an instant the sheriff hesitated, his anger apparently almost getting the better of him, but he controlled himself and when he spoke his voice was quietly level.

'Mebbe I was sorta quick,' he admitted, 'and mebbe I didn't have no reason to be that-a-way, but I happen to know the brand of them steers—they're Lazy W dogies—and I'm purty shore you don't work for that spread. So it's up to you to 'splain satisfactory how you come to be hazin' 'em 'long this trail what leads to Mexico.'

In that instant Walt Lee, shrewd judge of men, realized that Sheriff Watt Rice was a man with whom to reckon. Also that he was far more dangerous now when his voice was a silky purr than in his previous moment of bluster. He gathered quickly, too, that the men who rode with the sheriff were familiar with his moods and could be counted on to follow his lead without hesitation or bungling. Altogether, the Dark Rider knew he was in a tough spot. Suspicion still shone out of the eyes of the sheriff's men—suspicion that would swiftly be changed to action. The sheriff's brawny hand was swinging carelessly over his cut-out holster which, Walt noted, was tied down at the bottom.

Walt did not wish to reveal his identity to the sheriff, at least not yet. Nor to anybody, for that matter. Least of all to the officer's following, who might be duly sworn deputies or, most anything else. The Dark Rider was not much on talk; he usually preferred to act first and talk afterward. He acted now.

His slim, bronzed hands moved in a swift blurr that the eye scarce could follow. One instant they were empty, lying loosely against his thighs; the next they were filled with death. The black muzzles of his big sixes yawned hungrily at the sheriff and his posse.

'*Elevate!*'

The sheriff and his men did not hesitate. The Dark Rider's voice was like the crackle of a steel-bound lash. His slitted eyes were cold as the frozen emptiness of a dead hand glimmering under ice. Each man felt himself singled out by their bleak stare, and acted accordingly. Six pairs of hands shot into the air, and stayed there.

Sheriff Rice spoke, his voice soft and deadly—

'Feller, you can't get away with it!'

Walt's instant reply surprised and confused the posse almost as much as had his lightning draw.

'I know it,' he said, 'and I ain't gonna try to; but I am gonna have you fellers listen to what I have to say 'fore you turn yore wolf loose. If I hadn't pulled, you would have, and a hombre don't sound very convincin' when he's talkin' into the muzzle of a hawgleg—not near so as when he's talkin' in back of a coupla them. Fust thing, if you hadn't done made up yore minds 'fore you really knowed anythin' for shore 'bout what was goin' on, you'd a noticed that them dogies is headed *away* from Mexico. That oughta make even a petickler thickheaded gent think. Jest keep that in mind while I'm talkin'.'

Tersely, clearly, wasting no words, he recounted the happenings in the mesquite thicket. At first the posse showed interest and a willingness to be convinced; but as the tale unfolded, unbelief spread across their faces. One gave a low whistle as Walt finished.

'And you mean to set there and say you downed five Yaqui wideloopers all by yourself?' demanded the sheriff increduously.

111

'Feller, you shore tell 'em high wide and handsome, I'll say that for you!'

'It don't make sense nohow,' declared a lanky individual with a swarthy face and stooping shoulders

'All you got to do is ride a coupla miles to that thicket and see for yorself,' Walt told him calmly. 'You'll find four dead Injuns, that's certain. I callate the fifth one's prob'ly got well enough to hightail by now.'

'Another of the possemen spoke, a slim, quiet man with high cheekbones and blond hair bleached almost white by long years of Texas sun.

'My puhsonal 'pinion,' he stated, 'is that yuh're runnin' a whizzer, stranger. 'Twould be plumb nice—for you—if we went joggin' down the trail and left you to streak it any way you took a notion to go. Nacherly we wouldn't find no mesquite thicket fulla dead Injuns, but that wouldn't matter to you. Nope, stranger, that yarn of yore's is sorta leaky.'

'S'pose you send one or two of yore men to check up on me while the rest hang 'round here with me, Sheriff,' Walt suggested.

'Splittin' us up is playin' plumb inter his hands,' objected a squat, broad-shouldered man directly behind the sheriff.

The sheriff's face was angry and puzzled. Heedless of the menace of Walt's Colts, apparently forgetting all about them, he pulled his wide hat from his head and rumpled his hair—hair yellow as sunny gold and worn so long as to almost touch his shoulders.

Walt made no move at the sheriff's absentminded gesture, but there was a flicker of light in his green eyes and a slight tightening of his firm lips.

'Damn if I know what to do!' growled the sheriff, cuffing his hat back on his head and instinctively jerking his hands up as one of the Ranger's guns jutted forward a trifle.

The possemen shifted uneasily in their saddles and there was a low muttering that Walt could not catch. Something else had caught his attention, something that promised to tremendously complicate the situation.

Over a rise a few hundred yards behind the posse two riders suddenly loomed. As they swept down the slope, Walt swore softly under his breath. The foremost was undoubtedly a girl.

The sheriff and the posse heard the clatter of the swift hoofs. Their gaze slanted over their shoulders. Suddenly the rearmost man swore excitedly.

'Now we'll get the straight of this!' he bawled exultantly. 'Here comes Miss Betty herself and old Jake Nesbit.'

The Dark Rider's cold voice bit through the abrupt babble of talk.

'Steady!' he cautioned. 'You gents is still covered!'

Up to the posse swept the two riders. The

113

girl, Walt noted, was slim and tiny, with great dark eyes, and dark glossy hair that showed in wayward curls under the edge of her broad-brimmed hat. She sat her sturdy little pinto with willowy grace and the naturalness of the born rider. Her red lips were parted slightly in an expression of astonishment. Her companion was a rangy old fellow with a leathery face and grin wrinkles about his eyes. For some reason Walt could not fathom, he appeared intensely amused at the spectacle Sheriff Rice and his posse afforded.

'Posin' for a pitcher or somethin', Rice?' he drawled cheerfully as the oddly assorted pair pulled up at a little distance from the embarrassed posse.

'What in the world is going on?' demanded the girl in a silvery voice.

Sheriff Rice's handsome face flushed deeply and he shot a wrathful glance at Walt from his cold eyes. His voice, however, was level.

'Miss Betty,' he asked, 'd'you happen to know how yore steers come to be down here off yore spread? Looks to me like it's the trail herd you were gettin' together.'

'It is,' the girl replied instantly. 'Jake and I were trailing it, but we didn't have much hope of catching up with it. A band of Yaqui raiders rustled it out of the north range corral and drove it off. They shot Burley Gardner through the shoulder—thought they'd killed him, I guess. Burley managed to get to the ranchhouse and tell us what had happened. Did you take them from the Indians?'

The sheriff growled something that was certainly not a prayer. He ignored the question and asked one of his own—

'You say it was Injuns what run 'em off? Waren't no white men with 'em?'

'Five Yauis, Burley said,' the girl returned. 'Burley watched them ride off with the herd. He didn't say anything about white men.'

Her dark eyes turned wonderingly to the grim figure of the Dark Rider lounging carelessly in the saddle, his rock-steady guns still menacing the posse. She opened her lips to ask a question but the sheriff's harsh growl drowned the words

'I guess you win, feller,' he told Walt with no very good grace. 'It was a funny soundin' yarn, but what Miss Weston says sorta backs you up. Callate we kinda owe you a apology.'

The others nodded solemnly. Walt slid his guns back into their sheaths.

'I'm plumb willin' to set right here with you, Sheriff, wile some of yore men rides down to that thicket and checks up on me,' he offered.

'Ain't necessary,' grunted the sheriff. 'You can go on 'bout yore business if you're a-mind to, whatever that is.'

'You can look me up over to the minin' town, if you're a-mind to,' Walt told him. 'I'll be hangin' round there till I locates me a job of work.'

'Will somebody please tell me what it's all about?' begged the girl. 'Who am I to thank for bringing my cattle back?'

'Reckon that long-legged jigger is it,' grumbled the sheriff surlily. 'Anyhow it was him had 'em in charge when we run onto him. That was the fust thing we knowed about it. We was headin' for Laska.'

'C'mon, you work dodgers,' he growled to the posse. 'We'll be late gettin' in now. Good evenin', Betty, I'll be ridin' over to see you 'fore long.'

The girl nodded rather shortly as the posse got under way. Its members nodded to the Ranger as they filed past, but with little warmth. The sheriff shot him a cold glance. Walt heard the old cowboy chuckle softly.

'Seems you sorta put a snarl in Rice's rope for him, feller,' he addressed Walt, his twinkling eyes following the sheriff's stiff back. 'But don't you go thinkin' he'll fergit it,' he added soberly. 'Rice ain't the fergittin' kind. He'll shore be lookin' out for a chance to hang somethin' on you.'

'*Please!*' begged the girl, 'won't *you* tell me what this is all about, Mr.—'

Walt supplied his name, bowing courteously and removing his hat from his black head.

'You heard my name used, Mr. Lee,' rejoined the girl, 'and this is Jake Nesbit, one of my riders.'

'The hull darn outfit, now that ol' Burley is

116

laid up for a spell,' grinned Nesbit, ducking his grizzled head.

'I'm still waiting to hear what happened,' reminded Betty Weston.

Walt told her, briefly, making light of the matter. Old Jake let out a soft whistle and eyed the tall Ranger with respect.

'No wonder you made Rice and his outfit sit up on their hind laigs and beg,' he remarked, 'and that ain't easy to do.'

'I want to thank you,' the girl said simply. 'That herd means a lot to me right now.'

'I didn't do nothin' but what I had to,' Walt told her, his green eyes suddenly sunny and his white teeth flashing startlingly white in his bronzed face. 'Them copper-colored gents didn't give me much choice. I was jest sorta lucky and the luck spilled over on you.'

'Uh-huh, your kind us'ally is lucky when them sorta rukuses bust loose,' commented old Jake dryly. 'Golly, I'd liked to have seed that scrap!'

'You'll ride to the Ranch with us and have supper, won't you?' invited Betty Weston. 'It's only a few miles by way of a short cut through the hills. I wish I could reward you more fittingly,' she added with a smile.

Walt Lee had been doing some swift thinking. The Lazy W ranch, he gathered, was within easy riding distance of both Laska and Willard, which fitted in nicely with his plans. He reached a decision before the girl had

117

ceased speaking.

'Ma'am,' he said, 'there's somethin' you can do for me, all right. I heerd you say yore other hand was laid up for a spell with a hole in his shoulder. I callate that leaves you short a rider, don't it? Well, I'm sorta needin' me a job of ridin' right now. S'posin' you sign me on with you till he's able to get 'round again?'

The girl flushed painfully. 'There's nothing I would like better,' she said, 'but I'll have to tell you—neither Jake here nor poor Burley have been paid the wages due them for several months. I'll not be able to pay them until I sell this herd and another.'

'Burley and me ain't got no use for money right now,' put in old Jake quickly. Walt grinned at him understandingly and nodded. He spoke to the girl.

'Why, Ma'am,' he said, 'I ain't pertickler in need of cash money right now either. I got me a few pesos saved up and if I can work for my keep till you get straightened out I'll be settin' purty. I've done it before. Ain't at all uncommon with small spreads what ain't got much of a backlog to cut from. S'posin' we settle it on terms?'

The girl hesitated, her cheeks still flushed. 'It would be a wonderful help,' she said impulsively. 'I really don't know how we are going to get on as it is. Yes, if you are satisfied with those terms I'll be glad to sign you, Mr. Lee.'

118

'Then that's settled,' exclaimed the Ranger heartily. 'And, Ma'am, folks I work for us'ally calls me "Walt".'

They shoved the dogies through the hills as the western sky was turning scarlet and gold and the sleepy-songs of birds were dripping little liquid beads of music from the thickets. Walt Lee, tailing the herd, drew something from an inner pocket and studied it earnestly. It was the strand of hair he had unwound from murdered Curt Gordon's sleeve button. The concentration furrow between his black brows was deep as he returned the strand to his pocket.

''Bout the same length,' he mused, visioning Sheriff Rice's golden mane, 'but ain't jest the right color—not quite. More of the color of that snake-eyed gent's what spoke his piece back there; but his was cut short. Don't make sense that the sheriff would be mixed up in such goin's-on, but it don't do to miss no bets. Long hair gets cut sometimes and I got a sorta notion the yaller kind might bleach out when it waren't on a head. May not mean much, but somethin' to think about.'

CHAPTER FOURTEEN

DEVILS OF BLACK ROCK CANYON

Burley Gardner was short and broad as old Jake was long and lanky. He had a high, squeaky voice strangely in contrast to Jake's deep rumble. His shoulder wound was painful but not serious and had been expertly bandaged by the Mexican cook, who, Walt decided, was at least a hundred years old, possibly more, judging from the appalling number of wrinkles seaming her leathery face the color of well used saddle leather.

The old puncher squealed his delight at learning of the fate of the raiders.

'Yuh'd oughta busted the last one's haid with a rock, though,' he declared. 'Them varmints oughta be stomped on like a snake!'

The Mexican woman could cook, and Walt enoyed his supper. After the dishes were cleared away he talked with Betty Weston. The girl's story was simple.

'My father bought this little ranch when I was quite small,' she said. 'He did pretty well with it but he was chiefly interested in prospecting. He said there was gold in these hills and he was always trying to find it. He didn't, although others did. About four years ago he set out on one of his trips and that is the last I ever saw of him. Evidently he found what so many prospectors found, not gold, but a grave!'

There were tears in her dark eyes, but she quickly brushed them away and smiled into Walt's sympathetic face. 'I've tried to run the ranch since then,' she went on, 'but it has been a hard task. Jake and Burley, who worked for my father before I was born, have helped me hold it together—I could never have got along at all if it hadn't been for them.'

'Callate you sorta overest'mate things, Betty,' deprecated old Jake. 'Me and Burley needed a place to hang our ropes, thass all.'

Burley Gardner, propped up with pillows in a big chair, nodded his shining bald head in agreement and squeaked a blistering oath as a twinge shot through his shoulder. Betty shook her head.

'Things have been going badly of late,' she said. 'I'm afraid we can't hang on much longer if they don't change.'

'It looks like a mighty nice little spread to me,' Walt commented. 'This is a good range, Ma'am. I don't see no reason why it hadn't oughta pay.'

'The range is all right,' admitted the girl, 'but there are other things with which we have to contend. Time after time we have had cattle stolen, sometimes a whole herd, as today. We have had grass fires. Burley and Jake have been shot at. Last month we had a barn

121

burned and last winter we lost two hay stacks the same way. You see, the gold strike caused Laska to be built and brought in a very evil element. It also helped to revive the smuggling along the Sanlucar Trail, which runs through Black Rock Canyon not far from here. All kinds of lawless characters use that trail and they prey on the small ranches.'

Old Burley squeaked a word—'Uh-huh, and there's wuss than them in that canyon,' he declared. 'There's devils in it.'

'Huh?' Walt stared at the wounded puncher.

'Yeah,' declared Burley, 'there is; I've seed 'em—one of 'em, anyhow.'

'I callate it come outa a bottle of Bull Barty's hooch,' said Jake Nesbit, 'but you can't get him to admit it.'

'You're a liar,' squealed Burley. 'I hadn't had a drink all day. I was ridin' through Black Rock late one evenin', jest as it was gettin' dark,' he continued, addressing himself to Walt. 'I was jest passin' one of them narrer, crooked side canyons—there's a million of 'em runnin' inter Black Rock—and I seed this devil standin' there in the shadders squintin' at me. His eyes was big and black and he had a face jest as yaller as gold. My cayuse got scared and started swallerin' his haid. Then that devil let out a screech and turned 'round and flew up the canyon inter the dark.'

'You mean he run fast?' Walt asked.

122

'Nope, I don't,' disagreed Burley. 'I said flew, and flew he did. He jest went skimmin' along low 'bove the ground with his big wings flappin' up and down like a bat's. And that ain't the wust of it!'

Burley's squeak sank to a creaky whisper and Walt saw with astonishment that the old cowboy's face was beaded with sweat and his gnarled hands were shaking. 'No, that ain't the wust,' he repeated. 'The damn thing had a tail!'

'A tail!'

'Uh-huh, it stuck out behind him, longer'n my arm!'

Walt stared at Burley. His glance shifted to old Jake and the girl.

'You can't get him to change it,' said Nesbit resignedly, shrugging his shoulders.

'Burley undoubtedly saw something,' the girl admitted gravely. 'I don't believe in devils of the sort he describes, but there are plenty worthy of the name in those canyons.'

'If that waren't a *real* one I saw I ain't wantin' to see one,' twittered the old waddie pettishly.

'I betcha them hellions what robbed the bank last week had somethin' to do with it,' growled Nesbit. 'Ain't a bit o' doubt but that's the same outfit what's been raisin' hell around here for better'n a year. They got the stage twice, each time with a bullion shipment from the mines. That bank job was a big one. They

123

killed the cashier. And,' he added, lowering his voice instinctively, 'I betcha it was them what killed the Ranger.'

'Killed the Ranger?' prompted Walt.

'Uh-huh. There was a Texas Ranger had his headquarters in Laska. Mawnin' after the bank rob'ry he was picked up dead in a alley back of Bull Barty's saloon, the *El Dorado.* Somebody'd stuck a knife in his back. Sheriff rounded up a lotta greasers and other gents what was knowed to be handy with steel, but he couldn't pin nothin' on any of 'em. We been callatin' there'd be a troop of Rangers show up 'round hereabouts, but there ain't so far. Reckon they're too busy with the Injun trouble over to the west.'

'Nobody got any idea who the outfit is what has been raisin' the corners hereabouts?' Walt asked.

Old Jake shifted uncomfortably. 'Folks what have got curious or done loose talkin' has sorta had bad luck,' he replied evasively.

Walt nodded, understanding the old waddie's hesitancy. After all he, Walt, was a stranger. Talking carelessly in his presence might be anything but good policy. He was about to make a remark that would change the subject and put Nesbit at his ease when his keen ears caught a faint, staccato sound that was unmistakable. A moment later the others also heard it.

'Somebody comin',' squeaked Burley.

'Comin' darn fast, too,' rumbled Nesbit. 'Jest listen to that cayuse pound sand!'

Another minute passed and Betty Weston exclaimed in surprise:

'They're turning off the trail and coming this way!'

Old Jake slowly got to his feet, thumbs hooked over his cartridge belt.

'Sounds like they's jest one,' he drawled, 'but we ain't takin' no chances. Sorta onnacheral for a hombre to be splittin' the wind like that after dark. He's pullin' up in front the porch.'

Boots thudded up the steps and across the veranda. A hand pounded on the door and then flung it open. Into the room strode Sheriff Watt Rice, his handsome face black with anger, a dangerous light in his cold eyes. He halted just inside the door, glaring at Walt.

'Callated I'd find you here,' he rasped, his white and pointed teeth showing under his snarling upper lip. 'I don't know jest what kinda game you're playin', feller, but it shore don't look good. *We looked that thicket over from end to end and there waren't nary sign of a dead Injun in it!*'

CHAPTER FIFTEEN

THE SHERIFF'S PLAY

Walt Lee was rolling a cigarette with the slim fingers of one hand. Over the little white cylinder of paper and tobacco his level green eyes never left the sheriff's face. Not until the brain tablet was finished did he speak, his voice soft and drawling:

'Well, what 'bout it?'

'Jest this,' bawled the sheriff. 'You're goin' to the county seat with me and get locked up!'

'Uh-huh? Got a warrant?'

'Warrant for what?' roared Rice.

'That's jest what I'd like to know,' Walt told him calmly. 'Jest what charge were you figgerin' on puttin' 'gainst me?'

'Why—why—' stuttered Rice, his face purple.

Walt Lee rose to his feet with the lithe grace of a stalking panther. Tall as he was, Watt Rice had to raise his eyes slightly to meet the Ranger's level green gaze. His hand gripped the butt of his heavy Colt, but Walt Lee made no move and his slim fingers rested carelessly against the sides of his thighs. His quiet voice, all the softness gone out of it, cut through the sheriff's angry splutter like a steel blade through milk clabber.

'Rice,' he said, 'you're bellerin' through yore hat. You ain't got a single thing to 'rest me for, much less hold me on. If you can get Miss Weston to put a charge 'gainst me for rustlin' her cattle, you'll have somethin' to act on. If you can't, you're jest makin' big medicine yoreself puhsonal, and yore sheriff's 'thority don't cover that.'

'I got all the 'thority I need right here,' snarled the sheriff, jiggling his gun butt.

Walt glanced contemptuously at the holster tip bound tight to the sheriff's leg.

'I never knowed anybody what tied down to live very long,' he said. Suddenly his voice lashed at the sheriff—

'Rice, you ain't got enough 'thority there to back down a sick coyote, and you know it. You may be used to runnin' things highhanded in this neck of the woods, but don't try to be big skookum he-wolf with me 'less you're prepared to back yore play to the limit; and when you do that, don't hide behind that tin dishpan you're wearin'. If you're goin' to be a peace officer, be one. If you callate on settin' up as a gun slinger, leave yore badge to home. Now ask Miss Weston if she wants to put a charge 'gainst me.'

'I certainly do not!' exclaimed the girl before the sheriff could speak. 'Watt Rice, I think you are acting like a spoiled child. I'll wager the reason you didn't find those dead raiders is because you didn't look in the right

127

place for them. It would be just like you to run into the first thicket you come to and never stop to think whether it was the right one or not!'

For a moment the angry sheriff could not speak. He swallowed convulsively, drew a deep breath and finally managed to get words out—

'You—you takin' up for this range tramp! What's he to you?'

'He is my foreman,' the girl replied calmly. 'I hired him this afternoon.'

'Lots o' bus'ness you got with a foreman,' sneered the sheriff. 'Why you can't even pay—'

Splat!

Walt's open hand lashed out and took the sheriff squarely across the mouth, sending him reeling back with blood spurting from his cut lips. For an instant he sagged against the wall, his face dead white, his eyes flares of blue flame. Walt Lee stood perfectly still, his slim hands hanging loosely by his sides, his knees slightly bent.

For a long moment the sheriff stood with his right hand clamped on the butt of his Colt. In his eyes Walt read nothing of fear, only intense calculation. Finally his hand dropped from the gun. He shook his head and wiped his bloody lips.

'Nope,' he said thickly, 'I know a quick-draw man when I see one. I wouldn't have a chance. Callate that's jest what you're lookin' for—an excuse to throw down on me and then claim self defense. I've seed yore kind before—they us'ally hire out for jest such jobs as this. You can tell the fellers what sent you here that it didn't work; and don't think this is finished. You'll slip, sooner or later, and then it'll be the last deal for you. I admit I ain't got nothin' on you right now—as a sheriff, seein' as nobody will lay a charge—but there's plenty puhsonal 'tween us, and *that'll* be settled too, when the time comes.'

'I'll be there—when the time comes,' Walt told him.

The sheriff nodded. 'Sorry this hadda happen, Betty,' he said. 'I jest got yore best int'rests in mind, is all. Be seein' you!'

He stepped through the still open door, closing it after him. A moment later his horse's swift hoofbeats died away in the night.

Old Jake drew a deep breath. 'Well,' he said, 'that's the fust time I ever seed anybody make Watt Rice take water!'

Walt Lee gravely shook his head. 'He didn't take water, Jake,' he told the cowboy. 'He jest saw his hand waren't strong 'nough right now to set in the game. So he chucked inter the discard and rared back to wait for a new deal. His kind don't scare; but he don't go off half-cocked either. Which is somethin' to think 'bout.'

Later, as he lay on a narrow but comfortable bed in the bunkhouse, across the room from old Jake, Burly Gardner sleeping in

129

the ranchhouse where the ancient Mexican woman could keep an eye on him, Walt stared into the darkness very thoughtfully.

'It was a purty good play, sheriff,' he apostrophized Watt Rice, 'but you overdid it a mite. You was too het up at fust, and cumin' by yoreself waren't good jedgement, either. You ain't no fool and you knowed you didn't have a thing to hold me on—you showed that by cumin' 'thout yore posse. You didn't even go to the trouble to make yore yarn sound convincin' to me—you didn't care whether you fooled me or not. What you had in mind was to turn folks here against me. But why? That needs answerin'. Well, what with devils with tails, mysterious riders what nobody wants to talk about, sheriffs on the prod, and such, looks like this bus'ness is gonna be sorta int'restin'.'

A little later he reached up to where his shirt hung on a peg and fumbled something from the buttoned pocket. It was the bit of gold ore he had found in dead Michael Hubbell's coat. His slim fingers touched the rough surface speculatively.

'Now if *this'll* jest tie in somewhere,' he mused. 'Ain't so onreasonable to think it might. Hubbell was killed 'bout four years ago. Waren't much after that 'fore gold was struck in this section and Laska commenced buildin'. If somebody killed Hubbell for his claim, it stands to reason that the killer worked it. I

130

un'stand that there's a dozen payin' mines 'round Laska. Any one of 'em might be the one pore Hubbell stumbled onto. Of coh'se it looks darn funny that he would be amblin' round in the desert nigh onto fifty miles nawtheast of where he made his strike; but you never can tell 'bout desert rats—most of 'em is *loco* in some way or other. For some reason he mighta decided to file his location notice in Franklin. Well, all that's a lotta guessin', and anyhow, I got other things to hand right now.'

His slim fingers reached out and caressed the checkered grip of Curt Gordon's gun—the gun of vengeance!

CHAPTER SIXTEEN

HELL'S KETTLE

Walt's initial opinion that the Lazy W was a good spread was quickly confirmed to his own satisfaction. It was well watered, the grass was excellent and there were plenty of groves and canyons where the cattle could find shelter from sun, wind and storm. In some of those sheltered canyons little snow would fall even during the worst blizzards, which was an important item.

'Callate you don't hafta lay up much hay for winter,' he remarked to Jake Nesbit, who was 'showing him over' the ranch.

'Nope, we don't,' replied the oldtimer. 'If it waren't for wideloopin' and sich, this spread would make good money. Tom Weston was allus gallivantin' off lookin' for gold in the hills. If he'd stayed put and 'tended to the spread, he'd got rich 'fore the strike over to Laska started all the hell raisin' hereabouts and busted the cattle bus'ness.'

'Some fellers jest nacherly got the travel itch and hafta move 'bout,' Walt explained. 'They think they're lookin' for gold, but they ain't. It's t'other side of hills they're lookin' for.'

Old Jake eyed him speculatively. 'Got a notion you sorta like to peek over the top yoreself now and then,' he remarked sagely. 'You don't look to me like a feller what sots down and lets the grass grow onto the seat of his britches.'

Walt grinned and changed the subject.

'That sheriff seems a sorta competent feller,' he commented. 'Why don't he bust up this hellraisin' 'round here?'

'He's busted plenty,' old Jake admitted. 'Hung a dozen Mexicans in the past year and blowed quite a few Yaquis from under their hats. Org'nazation from up New Mexico way ambled down and started op'rations in this section. Watt and his dep'ties ran 'em inter the hills, surrounded 'em and downed ev'ry last one of 'em. Watt works fast, but there's some gents hereabouts what is faster'n him. There's

132

a mighty shrewd and salty outfit hangin' out somewhere in them hills, feller.'

A little later the old puncher turned his horse sharply to the north, toward where the strangely colored hills glowered under a coppery sky.

'Wanta show you somethin',' he said. 'That's Watt Rice's Flyin' Y,' he added, jerking his head to the west. 'T'other side his spread a coupla miles is Laska.'

For half an hour they rode north with the gaunt hills looming closer and closer. Walt could now see that the range was in the shape of a rough crescent, the western horn of which swept south around the site of Laska, its tip the weird jumbles of buttes and crags that formed the strange badland ridge across the face of the desert and extended to the very banks of the Rio Grande.

They climbed the first long slopes and reached a jagged rimrock.

'That's her,' said old Jake, gesturing widely with a sinewy hand. 'That's Black Rock Canyon, and the Sanlucar Trail runs through her and on inter Mexico. In Black Rock it branches out and runs all d'rections. Only fellers what knows 'em use them forks. Gawd only knows where they all run. Main trail cuts up inter New Mexico. Down there's where Burley claims to hev seed devils. Yeah, there's a way down little further west o' here. We use the Trail as a shortcut inter Laska, sometimes.

She ain't so nice ridin', 'cause you never can tell what you're gonna meet up with in there.'

Walt stared at the great gash in the hills. It was as if an angel's sword of vengeance had missed its stroke and slashed this ominous wound in the wantonly colored hills, and left it black with dried blood.

For black was the color of the canyon. All around it cliff and rock spire flung a shattered rainbow of flaming hues against the unresisting sky. Here the somber stone would have none of their hard gaiety. The hills were drunken harlots sneering at destiny, but the ominous canyon was a hypocritically penitent 'sister' who had donned sackcloth and ashes. The sneer was still there, but it lacked the saving grace of rich beauty for a background. The fangs of stone that jutted up from the canyon floor were like splintered, discolored teeth in a festering jawbone.

'Gosh, what a hole!' muttered the Ranger.

'Ain't no wonder Burley thought he saw the devils down there,' nodded Jake.

'After lookin' at it, I'm half in the notion of b'lievin' he did,' declared Walt. 'While you're at it, show me the way down there; might want to use it sometime.'

A little later they pulled up beside a winding incline that tumbled wildly down the steep wall of the canyon. It could be negotiated, by a good horse and a rider who knew his business, but it was no cure for weak nerves.

Walt suddenly swayed low over Goldy's neck to peer into the gorge. Even as he did so he felt a blast of wind fan his neck and heard the snapping crackle that sounds like nothing in the world but what it is—a high-power rifle bullet splitting the air. He also heard the queer little sound old Jake made as he slumped forward onto his horse's neck. Then the hard, metallic crash of the report slammed up from the shadows of the canyon.

Walt was off his horse, rifle in hand before the echoes had fairly begun to fling back and forth between the rock walls. Then, almost in the same move, he was back in the saddle, reining Goldy around, shouting to him.

Old Jake was riding a nervous piebald just off pasture. When he slumped forward, his right spur tangled in the stirrup strap and as the cayuse leaped with fright the sharp rowel jabbed him in the ribs. With each move the old man's body swayed and the horse got another painful jab. Snorting with pain and anger he plunged along the rim of the canyon. Swiftly his anger turned to uncontrollable panic. Madly he fled along the edge of the crumbling rim. Ahead of him, less than half a mile distant, a short box canyon slashed through Black Rock's wall. Its edge was fringed with thick brush. Toward this masked death trap scudded the frantic piebald, heedless of all but a desire to escape the devilish thing that jabbed and raked his sensitive ribs.

Behind him the great sorrel skimmed across the ragged stones, belly hugging the ground, legs working like pistons. Despite the piebald's start he closed the distance between them swiftly. Walt urged him on with voice and hand, his gaze flickering from old Jake's drunkenly swaying body to the fringe of bush that fairly raced toward him. Nesbit might be dead, but Walt was not sure. There seemed to be an instinctive leg grip holding the cowboy in the saddle.

'Get him, boy! Get him!' Walt urged the sorrel. Goldy snorted, and poured his big body over the ground. Inch by inch he closed the gap. His straining nose reached the piebald's haunch, his flank. Walt leaned forward, tense, ready. Goldy's flaring nostrils blew foam against Nesbit's leg. Walt lunged ahead, arms outstretched, just as the piebald crashed through the brush fringe and with a human scream went rolling and summersaulting down the almost perpendicular, boulder-studded slope. A wild snort, a prodigious clashing of hoofs and Goldy too plunged over the lip!

CHAPTER SEVENTEEN

DEATH STRIKES

By a miracle of balance the sorrel kept his feet, Walt guiding him as best he could with knees and voice. In the last mad instant he had snatched old Jake from the saddle and was holding him cradled across his own broad breast. Leaning forward, keeping his balance only by the mighty grip of his straining thighs, he managed to pick up the hanging reins from Goldy's neck.

Walt's firm grip on the reins helped the golden horse immeasurably. It renewed his confidence, steadied his floundering legs. Boulders loomed before him, loose stones rolled beneath his shoes; but, snorting and blowing he skidded and zigzagged down the treacherous slope. More and more stones were knocked free; patches of loose earth joined them. In a cloud of dust, riding the rear of a miniature avalanche, Goldy finished the last hundred yards 'sittin' on his tail.' A last mighty snort, a shower of sparks from steel-shod hoofs and he hit the canyon floor in a final magnificent skitter, clawed his way out of the dust cloud and came to a panting halt on a patch of lush green grass.

Cr-r-r-rack!

For the second time that day, Walt Lee left his saddle like a thrown spear. Almost in the same marvel of motion he dropped old Jake's limp form onto the soft grass and hauled his rifle from the boot. Weaving, ducking, his saddlegun streaming fire, he raced across the canyon floor, bullets snapping and crackling about him. The man who had fired the treacherous shot from behind a boulder leaped away from his useless shelter and crouched low, gun barrel lining with the Ranger's broad breast.

Shot after shot Walt hurled at him, ejecting the spent shells in a flashing blur of motion. Had the rifle jammed, the lever would have splintered like matchwood.

He saw the drygulcher reel back, steady himself, try to take aim. Walt slammed a stream of lead at the flash of his belt buckle. The other went down, sprawling, limbs a-twitch. He half turned on his side, tried desperately to raise his rifle and sank back, shuddered once and was still.

Walt straightened up, the smoking Winchester still held ready. He raised one steady hand and shoved his hat back from his eyes.

'Feller, you shore took a lot of killin',' he nodded to the dead drygulcher.

For a moment he stood sweeping the canyon from wall to wall with his keen gaze. He saw nothing, heard nothing other than the brawl and brabble of swift water. Evidently the would-be murderer had been alone. Still alert, he walked up to the sprawled body.

The man, a lean, sinewy individual, lay with his face plainly in view. His hat had fallen off, revealing thin, light hair growing unevenly on a big head. His glazing, half-open eyes were a pale blue. Walt gazed at him, a perplexed expression on his bronzed face.

'Feller, I know I ain't never seed you before,' he mused, 'but you shore do remind me a heap of somebody I seen plumb recent. Now jest who, I wonder?'

Behind him a voice suddenly spoke—

'Trail's end, pardner!'

Walt stewed around to face old Jake Nesbit, who was coming toward him rather groggily. There was a smear of blood on the puncher's face and a red furrow high up through his gray hair. He had evidently been neatly creased by the drygulcher's bullet and knocked unconscious.

'Yeah,' he repeated, 'trail's end for that jigger. I don't know jest what happened, but I got a notion it was darn near trail's end for you and me. I see my bronk is back there in the rocks with a busted neck. Callate you kept me from goin' over the rim with him, didn'tcha? Looks like I'm sorta in yore debt.'

'You got Goldy to thank, not me,' Walt told him. 'If that yaller hellion waren't a cross 'tween a tomcat and a flyin' squirrel, we'd both have them rocks up along there greased so slick a fly couldn't crawl up 'em. B'lieve me, that hoss is a wonder!'

The sorrel came trotting at his whistle and thrust his velvety muzzle into Walt's hand. The Ranger tweaked his ears affectionately and Goldy tried to nip off the end of his nose in return.

'He's either savin' my life or tryin' his damndest to kill me,' Walt told Nesbit. 'You know that punctured gent there?' he asked, jerking his head toward the stiffening body.

'Never seed him before,' replied old Jake. 'Why in hell you reckon he tried to plug me? I ain't never done nothin' to nobody what I can recall. Leastwise nuthin' what would call for a killin'.'

'Callate he sorta nicked you by accident,' Walt replied. 'He pulled trigger jest as I leaned over. If I'd stayed settin' straight in my hull a split second longer he'd 'a drilled me dead centre. Musta had a bead drawed square 'tween my eyes.'

Old Jake stared at him for a moment, then hesitantly asked a question—

'You—you know anybody what would be in the notion of downin' you?'

Walt shrugged his wide shoulders. 'I done a heap o' ridin' in my time,' he replied evasively. 'I've knowed lots of fellers, and had run-ins with some of 'em. Some fellers have good mem'ries for faces, and good eyes.'

'Uh-huh' agreed Nesbit; 'and it ain't so far from down here up to the rimrock, for a feller with good eyes.'

Walt nodded. To himself he was saying: 'Outside of Jake, Burley Gardner and Miss Betty, there ain't but six gents what has even seed me in this deestrict—the sheriff and his outfit—and this cashed-in sidewinder ain't one of 'em! Jest what is the answer to this?'

The dead man's clothing disclosed nothing that lent a clue to his identity, although Walt searched him with Ranger thoroughness. After a final scrutiny of his pallid features, the Dark Rider turned away, the face indelibly stamped on his memory. He was still trying to place the resemblance which plagued him, but was unsuccessful. Finally he gave it up for the present.

With old Jake forking the sorrel, they picked their way up the dizzy track which led from the canyon floor to the rimrock. On the summit, Walt turned and gazed long and earnestly into the ominous gorge where the snaky Sanlucar trail slipped furtively along between the gloomy walls. Suddenly he asked the old cowboy an unexpected question—

'Jake, why was Watt Rice so on the prod when he heard Miss Betty say she'd hired me?'

Old Jake chuckled creakily. 'Well,' he replied, 'Watt don't hanker to have well-set-up, good-lookin' young fellers workin' on the Lazy W. You see, he's sorta sweet on Betty—

141

been tryin' to talk her inter marryin' him for quite a spell now.'

CHAPTER EIGHTEEN

HELL'S KETTLE BOILING

During the long ride back to the ranchhouse, Goldy carrying double, Walt was silent and distraught. Old Jake's amused answer to his question had exploded a theory that had been taking shape in his mind. It had provided a simple explanation for Sheriff Rice's peculiar actions. It began to appear that they, after all, were but the unreasonable outbursts of a madly jealous man whose suit with the lady of his choice was apparently meeting with scant success. Doubtless Rice had watched him ride off with Betty Weston in the wake of the recovered herd and had construed her interest in his, Walt's, explanation of what had happened as interest in Walt himself. The Ranger, who was far from being unattractive to women, had experienced something of the sort more than once before.

'Guess I'd better mosey over to that darn town and see what's to see there,' he decided as the ranchhouse loomed through the dusk.

He did ride for Laska the following evening, old Jake, his head bandaged and his disposition not the best, riding with him. Jake had in fact himself suggested the trip, there being necessary supplies to be ordered for the household.

'I wanta tell Watt Rice 'bout that shootin', anyhow,' he explained to Betty Weston. 'Too darn many funny things happen' 'round this neck o' the woods of late.'

They reached the outskirts of the mining town just as the lovely blue dusk was sifting down over the hills, softening their harsh colors and jagged outlines. Only a faint amber streak above the mountain tops remained of the sunset and in the western sky a single great star glowed and trembled. Even the gaunt ugliness of the town was subdued in the mild and chastening light of the dying day.

There was nothing to subdue the pandemonium of discordant sound that boiled up from the seething hell-kettle, however. It was apparent while the twinkling lights of Laska were still far off. It grew and strengthened as they approached. Its monotonous undertone was the ceaseless growl and rumble that was the accompaniment to the everlasting ponderous dance of the mighty stamps in the stamp mills. Hour after hour, through daylight and through dark, the great rods of iron, as thick as a man's ankle and heavily shod with a mass of iron and steel at their lower ends, rose and fell in an iron battery box; grinding the gold ore to powder. From the tireless dance of the stamps came the wealth that set the mad tempo of the mining town's carousal. Their steady roar was a fitting base for the blare of wild music, the thump of booted feet and the click of high heels that gushed through the swinging doors of dancehall and saloon. Above their low grumble sounded the click of roulette wheels, the chink of bottle neck against glass, the slither of shuffled cards. They beat the time to song, or what passed for it. Through the air they set a-quivering sliced the death scream of a man whose life gurgled out around the knife in his throat. Ceaselessly they churned the sticky paste of the powdered ore; and just as ceaselessly life in the raw churned and boiled and seethed and bubbled beneath the hot glow of the Texas stars. Laska was wild and woolly and didn't take any pains to conceal the fact.

Walt and Nesbit put their horses away and then moved, side by side through the colorful crowd that swarmed the crooked street. They rubbed shoulders with lithe young cowboys, booted and spurred, from the neighboring ranches. By them slipped swarthy Mexicans in velvet trimmed with silver, their gay *serapes* flung across their chests in graceful, sweeping fashion. *Senoritas* with dark, liquid eyes glanced approvingly at the Ranger's tall form, as did various ladies with too-red lips and too-bright eyes as he passed the open dancehalls. There was a reek of spilt whiskey in the saloons. Later there would also be the raw, piercing smell of spilt blood, and the acrid tang of burned powder.

'She's a humdinger, ain't she?' remarked old Jake.

'She shore is,' Walt replied. 'Can't say as I ever seed a saltier *pueblo*.'

'Callate here's where we might as well surround us a drink or two,' said Nesbit, turning into a saloon. 'This is the biggest and best and hell-raisin'est place in town—the *El Dorado*; Bull Barty runs her.

'Bull ain't very purty to look at,' he added as they shouldered their way to the bar, 'but he ain't a bad sort. It was Bull who fust struck gold in these hills. He staked a claim up nawth from here a piece. Was a almighty rich pocket, but it didn't last. Bull raked out a hefty poke of dust, though, workin' her by hand. Then she petered out. Meanwhile Perley Cooper had located his Monarch Mine down this-a-way, and Tom Fisher had struck the Root Hawg, and Blunt Workman was sinkin' a shaft in the Blue Peter. Bull he looks 'round, callated all the best ground had been located and does some mighty shrewd figgerin'. So he 'vested his poke in the El Dorado saloon and purty soon he had 'bout the best payin' "claim" in town. Of co'hse as other shafts was sunk and the town began growin', other places was opened up; but Bull was here fust and he still gets the best of the trade. All the big owners like Perley

145

Cooper and Fisher and Workman does most of their drinkin' here. They have some whoppin' big poker games in the back rooms, too, and Bull cuts in on that. Fellers like Cooper don't think much of Bull, but they spends their money here jest the same. Cooper is jest 'bout fust citizen—allus shellin' out money to improve things and helps lots of folk what need it. Bull helps folks, too, but he has a sorta leanin' toward greasers and dancehall gals and miners what get hurt, and sich like— the kind better folks don't 'zactly 'prove of. So they don't 'zactly 'prove of Bull, either.'

While he lent one ear to the garrulous Nesbit, Walt was examining the big saloon. To one side was a dancefloor upon which a swarm of cowboys and miners jigged and thumped to the music of a Mexican orchestra. They swung their silk-skirted partners lustily and bawled frequent choruses in time with the music, some of which should have been sung with discretion and some sung not at all. There was a row of poker tables, a couple of roulette wheels, a crap table, a faro bank and a monte game, all going full blast. The long bar was lined from end to end. Behind it a battery of sweating drink jugglers worked feverishly.

Arranging bottles on the back bar was a tall man with slightly graying hair. He turned around and it seemed to Walt he had never seen so hideous a face, for the eyes were of the palest yellow, the nose was broken and driven inwards, while the whole countenance was seared and puckered with scars. The lighter hue of his cheeks and lips told the Ranger that he was a man who had long worn a beard, although at present he was clean shaven. His gaze fell on Jake Nesbit and he nodded in a friendly fashion. The old cowboy beckoned him and he sauntered forward, extending a sinewy hand.

'Bull,' said Nesbit, shaking hands with unmistakable warmth, 'I wants you to know Walt Lee, who's workin' for the Lazy W now. Walt, this is Clarke Barty, better known as "Bull."'

Barty grinned, showing an excellent set of crooked white teeth.

'Pleased to meetcha, Lee,' he rumbled in a deep bass. His fingers closed over Walt's in a steely grip. 'How's the little lady, Jake?' he inquired of Nesbit.

Old Jake let out a string of crackling oaths and proceeded to regale the saloonkeeper with an account of the recent Lazy W mishaps, including the attempted drygulching in Black Rock Canyon. Barty regarded Walt with fresh interest and shook hands a second time.

'I heerd somethin' of a wideloopin' over there,' he said, 'but I didn't get no perticklers —ain't been able to run Watt Rice down. Lee, it shore seems you done yoreself proud. Have a round on the house, boys, coupla 'em. Be back with you in a little—got to see 'bout some

147

stock we're short of.'

He disappeared into one of the back rooms. The bartender set out bottles and glasses.

Walt sipped his drink thoughtfully, staring at the door which had closed behind Barty and hardly hearing old Jake's flow of chatter. Barty's coat had swung open, revealing a length of gold watch chain across his broad breast. Dangling from the chain was a peculiar charm—a bit of polished quartz with beads of gold showing thickly amid the rock, a specimen greatly resembling the rough fragment Walt Lee carried buttoned in his shirt pocket!

CHAPTER NINETEEN

GUN SMOKE

Bull Barty's whiskey was not noted for mildness. It went down the throat with a sizzling sound, hit the stomach and bounced. After the third drink, old Jake's countenance wrinkled in a leathery smile.

'She shore does warm yore innards,' he declared. 'This is what I call prime likker.'

'She's prime all right,' agreed Walt, 'primed with dynamite and cactus spines! Hello, here comes our friend the sheriff. Who's that with him?'

Nesbit glanced over his shoulder at the two men who had just pushed through the swinging doors.

'That's Perley Cooper, the big mine owner,' he said. 'Fine lookin' feller, ain't he?'

Walt agreed that Cooper was a striking looking man. Tall and straight, he had a wiry figure that denoted strength and endurance. His eyes were black, deeply set in his head. His cheek bones were high, his nose straight. He had a splendid beard, almost snow white, that rippled down over his broad breast. His age was uncertain—Walt judged him to be somewhere in the neighborhood of fifty but conceded that he might easily be five years older or younger. He and the sheriff moved across the saloon toward one of the back rooms, discussing something as they walked.

'Wouldn't be serprised if they're gettin' up a big poker game,' commented old Jake. 'Hang on here a minute, will you? I want to speak to Watt a minute 'bout that drygulchin'.'

He hurried across the room and halted the sheriff. Perley Cooper nodded agreeably. The sheriff listened with a frown, darted a look toward where Walt lounged carelessly against the bar and his frown deepened. Finally he grunted something, appearing to agree reluctantly with what old Jake was urging. Cooper asked the cowboy a question and spoke to Rice. Then the two of them passed through the back room door. Nesbit hurried back to Walt's side. 'Watt's gonna look inter it,' he said. 'Says he'll ride over there and see if he knows that hellion, that is if the coyotes ain't got him yet—they hadn't oughta, the way we wedged him in 'mong them rocks.'

'Sheriff didn't look pertickler pleased,' commented Walt.

'Nope, he didn't,' chuckled Jake. 'He said, "is that long-legged hellion allus gonna come out on top in ev-thin!"' Seemed sorta peeved 'cause you downed that jigger so easy. Cooper told him he waren't takin' enough int'rest in a crime what was committed. I don't think Watt liked that any too well either, but he won't arg'fy with Cooper. Look, there he comes now.'

Sheriff Rice passed out of the saloon without so much as a glance in the Ranger's direction. He appeared preoccupied and in a hurry.

A little later Bull Barty appeared. He joined Walt and Jake at the bar and they had a drink together.

'Purty nice place you got here, Mr. Barty,' Walt admired. 'Back rooms and ev'thin'.'

'Uh-huh,' conceded Barty, 'I sorta think so myself. Wanta look her over?' he invited.

Together they inspected the roulette wheels, poker tables and other games. Barty commented on the skill of the Mexican musicians and nodded pleasantly to the dancing girls nearby. The girls returned the nod

150

and eyed the tall Ranger with unmistakable favor. Walt paused in front of one of the back room doors.

'I use that one for private poker games and sich,' Barty explained, flinging open the door. 'See, there's another door. You can come in the back door of the buildin' and get in here by way of the hall. Makes it nice for gents what want to step in and play 'thout botherin' with the boys in the big room. Cooper and Blunt Workman and them fellers play in there every now and then. Sheriff Rice sets in sometimes, too, and his dep'ties and his ranch foreman and one or two of his hands.'

Walt opened the far door and glanced down the corridor.

'Does make it handy,' he conceded. He closed the door and his swift gaze traveled about the little room, missing nothing. He noted, among other things, a round cheese box filled with sawdust, which served as a spittoon for tobacco chewers. As Barty and old Lake turned to the door he did a peculiar thing. He stooped quickly, scooped up a handful of the sawdust from the box and dropped it in his coat pocket. Neither Nesbit nor Barty noticed the action.

Barty left them at the bar.

'We'll have one more and then callate we'd better be toddlin',' remarked old Jake. Walt nodded agreement. Glass in hand he stared into the big mirror of the back bar, watching the colorful play of movement reflected in the glass. Suddenly his gaze remained fixed and his eyes narrowed slightly in the shadow of his wide hat.

A man had just entered the room, a slim quiet looking man with pale, steady eyes and hair that was bleached almost white. Walt recognized him as a member of Sheriff Rice's posse on the day of his run in with the Yaquis. His eyes had swiftly searched the room and Walt knew that it was himself upon whom they had centered with an expression of malignant hatred. He tensed as the man's hand dropped to his side. Then in a single panther leap he was away from the bar, hurling old Jake to one side in the same movement.

'You damn murderer!' yelled the white-haired man as his gun roared.

The back bar mirror crashed in fragments. Men yelled wildly, women screamed. There was a frantic scramble to get out of range. The gunman swung his six around for a second shot that would not miss. Even as his fingers curled on the trigger, Walt Lee's big Colts streamed fire.

Grimly, relentlessly, he hammered the gunman with bullets. He felt the burn of a slug that seared his cheek, heard another yell over his shoulder. Then he stepped back, ejecting the empty shells from his guns and replacing them with fresh cartridges. Alert, ready, he stood beyond the drifting wisps of powder smoke, his icy green eyes flickering from the still form on the floor to the swirling, neck-craning crowd. Isolated shouts went up, some of them threatening.

'Anybody int'rested?' inquired the Ranger softly.

'No, they ain't!' rumbled a voice from near the bar. Bull Barty stood there, a sawed-off shotgun in his hands. Beside him stood Jake Nesbit with a ready colt.

'I saw the whole thing,' shouted Barty. 'Why in hell Whitey Davis tried to shoot this feller in the back I don't know, but that's jest what he did. This feller shot in self defense.'

'That's right,' shouted several other voices. 'We saw it, too.'

'Here comes the sheriff,' yelled somebody.

Sheriff Rice pushed through the swinging doors, ran his eye over the scene and frowned blackly as it rested on Walt.

'So yuh're inter it again, Lee,' he growled harshly, striding toward the Ranger. 'Hand them guns over—I'm puttin' you under 'rest.'

Before Walt could speak, Bull Barty stepped forward, shotgun cradled in the crook of his arm.

'Jest a minute, Watt,' he said. 'Yuh're sorta oversteppin' yoreself. I'm duly 'lected marshal of this town and I was here when the shootin' happened. I'm handlin' this case and I'm tellin' you right now there ain't a bit of sense in puttin' a charge 'gainst this feller. That rider of

153

yores musta gone plain *loco*. A dozen folks saw what happened and they'll every one swear that Lee acted in self defense. I'll swear it myself.'

Sheriff Rice drew along breath. He ignored Barty and glared at Walt.

'Still gettin' the breaks,' he said with deadly softness, 'but your time'll come, feller, it'll come!'

He turned to the dead man. 'Help me get him outa here,' he requested of several acquaintances. Together they carried the body from the saloon. A swamper swabbed up the blood and scrubbed the floor. The orchestra struck up a lively tune. Boots began to thump once more. The gamblers went back to their games. Bull Barty glanced gravely at Walt.

'Ev'body knows Whitey Davis was a killer,' he remarked, 'and 'cause of that there ain't nobody liable to pay much 'tention to what he yelled jest 'fore he pulled trigger. If you and him had a run-in some time some place else and you don't wanta talk 'bout it, that's yore bus'ness; but don't fergit, Davis had friends. He rode for Watt Rice and Watt seemed to think sorta well of him. Watt won't fergit and them other Flyin' Y hellions won't fergit either. You wanta walk sorta easy and slow, feller.'

Walt thanked Barty for his advice and he and Jake left the saloon.

'Damn if this don't beat anythin' yet!'

declared the old puncher. 'Whitey was shore on the prod. If you hadn't moved like goose-greased lightnin', he'd a drilled you. Say, Bull Barty's a nice feller, ain't he?'

'Sorta acts that way,' Walt agreed. 'Wonder where he got that funny watch charm he wears?'

'Callate it's a piece of ore from his strike,' hazarded Nesbit. 'Lots of miners wear 'em for lucky pieces.'

Walt was long going to sleep that night. He lay quietly on his bunk, staring into the darkness, trying to fit together the jig-saw puzzle of the recent happenings. Finally he gave it up, for the time.

'Bull Barty aint got long hair, that's shore,' he mused as he turned over to go to sleep, 'but there's one thing I know now for jest 'bout certain. I know *where* Curt Gordon was killed!'

CHAPTER TWENTY

DEVILS DINE

Six men sat at a table in one of the back rooms of Bull Barty's saloon. Cards were on the table, and money, but they were not playing. The lamps were turned low and the room was shadowy. The man who sat with his back to one of the locked doors was speaking. His hat

155

was pulled down over his eyes and the lower part of his face was but a whitish blur in the shadows.

'Well, what have you jiggers got to s'gest?' he asked.

An inarticulate growl went 'round the table. 'That long-legged hellion shore has raised hell and put chunks under the corners since he lit in this section,' rasped a gangling, swarthy man. 'Whitey and his brother both kilt and that little wideloopin' all smeared. There's hell b'low the Line over at last, gents. Old Chief Metzla is bellerin' his haid off 'bout his four bucks gettin' cashed in, and wantin' to get paid for it.'

'Let him beller!' grunted another of the group.

'We need Metzla and his riders,' differed the first speaker. 'They're a lotta help in shovin' stuff 'crost the Line.'

'What I wanta know,' grumbled the gangling man, 'is how come Whitey's brother missed that hellion clean after he'd drawed a bead on him; Brand Davis was s'posed to be quite a hand with a long gun.'

'Mostly luck, chances are,' remarked a broad-shouldered, stocky individual. 'What *I* wanta know is who is that galoot, and where did he come from?'

The man with the low-drawn hat spoke "softly"—Ain'tcha got no idea?'

'No I ain't. Puhsonally I got a notion it'd be

a good idear to try and sign him up. He's shore a whizzer. He—'

'What happened in this room the night the bank was cleaned?' interrupted the other.

Dead silence greeted the remark; there was an uncomfortable shifting of feet.

'A Ranger died here,' went on the speaker. 'Died so you bunglers wouldn't do a dance on nothin' lookin' up a rope. You s'pose the Ranger outfit is gonna let that pass? We callated there was liable to be a troop ridin' up this way. Ain't no troop showed up, but this big quickdraw gent with eyes like smoky ice *does* show up from nowhere. The things he's did since he lit here are jest the sorta things a tophand with that outfit is s'posed to do. Of co'hse our sheriff might be right—mebbe he *is* jest a tough hombre on the scoot from New Mexico or Oklahomy—*mebbe!*'

Another silence followed. 'What we gonna do 'bout it?' queried a voice at length.

The first speaker stared coldly. He said nothing, but his sinewy hand made a sweeping gesture. Again there was an uncomfortable shuffling of feet.

'Killin' Rangers is a mighty bad bus'ness,' observed the gangling man with the drooping moustache. 'Sooner or later they allus git you.'

'But we're sorta like the feller what got the bear by the tail,' observed the chunky man. 'He wanted to let go, but he dasn't. We're all in this bus'ness so damn deep there ain't no

157

pullin' out for nobody.'

Quick, furtive looks followed this remark. Glints of suspicion showed in hard eyes. The quiet leader's voice cut through the welter of distrust that was arising.

'Nobody's pullin' out,' he said. 'Nobody can 'ford to. Ev'thin's goin' on as us'al.'

'It's easy for you,' growled the gangling man. 'Yuh're settin' purty—it's us what takes the risks. You—'

His querulously complaining voice died in a choking gurgle. Against his throat was the point of a long, thin knife with an edge like a newly honed razor. The voice back of the shimmering blade was as deadly keen and ruthless as the cold steel—

'One more break like that outa you, Silver, and she rips. Gonna say it?'

The other swallowed convulsively and sat rigid, lips stiff, eyes bulging. The other waited a crawling moment and then flipped the knife out of sight as swiftly as he had drawn it.

''Nough of this,' he said quietly. 'We're all t'gether and that's all there is to it, like it or not. Now let's get t' work on that little bus'ness of the fifteenth. And don't ferget, that long-legged hellion is ev'body's job. I'll try and figger out somethin', but don't nobody let no chances slip.'

Walt Lee rode into Black Rock Canyon, alone. He wanted to give the sinister gorge a thorough going-over. For hours he prowled about amid the weird rock formations, investigating the numerous side canyons that opened into the main cleft. Most of them were shallow box canyons, but now and then a narrow slash crawled crookedly through the hills for miles. At times he encountered faint trails, some of them showing evidence of recent usage. It was near dusk when he stumbled on a narrow opening in the main canyon wall almost concealed by a bristle of chaparral. He halted Goldy and peered into the shadowy cleft. Suddenly he sniffed.

A tangy odor was drifting on the air. Watt instantly recognized it as the smell of wood smoke.

'Now what?' he muttered. 'Where's that comin' from? Outa that hole, shore as hell!'

Cautiously he guided Goldy into the cleft. There was a trail there, more plainly defined than many of the others he had noted during the day; but until the side canyon was actually entered, it was not apparent, due to the rocky formation outside the cleft. A moment later he was urging the sorrel into the thick growth which flanked the trail. To his ears, faint with distance, had come the uneven click of fast hoofs.

Tingling with interest he waited as the running clicks grew louder. He leaned forward, hand hovering over the sorrel's nose. Goldy was not given to promiscuous neighing, but Walt was taking no chances. A sudden lyric urge to intone a hymn to the evening star would be inconvenient just at present, to say the least. Goldy, however, stood motionless and silent as the hoofbeats drew near. A moment later Walt saw the shadowy form of the horseman pass his hiding place, headed for the mouth of the gorge. He remained listening until the hoofbeats had died away down the main canyon. Then he eased Goldy out of the thicket and paced him slowly up the gorge, into which very little light was filtering.

Several hundred yards of slow progress and he again headed the sorrel into a thicket. The smell of burning wood, intermingled with an appetizing odor of boiling coffee, was strong now. Walt dismounted, told Goldy to stay where he was, and stepped into the trail on foot. With the utmost caution he crept along in the shadows. He rounded a turn, peered through a screen of brush and clucked softly to himself.

Less than a score of yards distant was a big cabin built of logs, with a split-pole roof and a mud-and-stick chimney from which smoke was rising. A window, partially obscured by the branches of a low-growing tree which brushed against it, showed a golden square in the gloom. Walt could also see a stout plank door secured by a heavy padlock. To his ears came a low murmur.

'Now what the hell?' he wondered. 'This shore will stand some investigatin'.'

Flat on his belly in the tall grass he snaked forward, careful inch at a time. He reached the deep shadow of the tree growing beside the window, wormed his way to the log wall and cautiously raised his head to the level of the window ledge. For a long minute he stared into the big, crowded room, peering between the heavy iron bars which crisscrossed the window.

'So *them's* the devils Burley Gardner saw!' he murmured, listening to the high sing-song chatter that welled from the locked and barred room, the occupants of which were busily engaged in preparing their evening meal. His lips quirked in an amused grin. 'No wonder the old coot thought he was up against somethin',' he chuckled to himself, visualizing what the bald-headed puncher had seen in the shadows of the canyon mouth. 'Callate one of 'em musta busted loose or was a trusty or somethin' and wandered down there. Reckon Burley scared him 'bout as bad as he scared Burley.'

The mystery of the wings and tail of which Gardner had prated was also solved. Walt chuckled again at the thought of it, and stood up in the shadow of the tree.

'I'd better be hightailin' outa this 'fore that jigger comes ridin' back up the trail to keep a eye on that pack,' he decided.

The slightest of sounds started him turning around. He froze in the act as a cold circle

161

jabbed into the small of his back.

'*Seno*r, you will raise your hands and walk straight ahead,' said a harsh voice in halting Spanish.

CHAPTER TWENTY-ONE

YAQUI GUNS

Walt did as he was told. He had no choice in the matter, with that gun muzzle prodding his back.

'How in hell did that Jigger slip up behind me 'thout me hearin' him?' was his first amazed and disgusted reaction to his predicament.

A moment later, when he had stepped into the light of the moon, now pouring straight down into the canyon, he understood. A swift glance risked over his shoulder showed a dark, high-nosed face with piercing black eyes and black hair cut in a square bang across the low forehead. His captor was a Yaqui Indian, able to move with the silence of a drifting shadow. Doubtless, from some point of vantage, he had observed the Ranger's approach and, with true Indian stealth and caution, awaited his opportunity and silently closed in behind him to make the capture.

A hissed command brought the Ranger's

162

head around. An instant later his guns were jerked from their sheaths. A groping hand felt Curt Gordon's Smith & Wesson in the shoulder holster under his left arm. The Yaqui mumbled something that Walt did not understand and tugged at his buttoned coat.

During his adventurous career as a Texas Ranger, Walt Lee had been in more than one tight spot. Working lone handed as he did, he could seldom if ever count on outside assistance. He could depend only on his lightning-fast gun hands, his steely strength and his quick wits in moments of emergency. He knew this, and the knowledge made him doubly dangerous to men who believed they had him at an utter disadvantage. At the moment his hair-trigger mind was tensely alert to the slightest lessening of vigilance on the part of his captor. His trained muscles were ready for instant response.

The Yaqui had trouble with the coat buttons. Walt's hands were raised shoulder high and the Indian's wrist was between his loosely hanging upper arm and his side. He felt the gun muzzle waver a little as the other's fingers fumbled with the buttons. With the speed of light the Dark Rider acted.

His upper arm, rigid as a bar of steel, clamped the Indian's wrist. Simultaneously he hurled his body sideways, jerking the other off balance. The gun roared and he felt the searing burn of the bullet ripping along his

163

ribs. Before the other could pull trigger a second time, Walt had whirled clear around and gripped the gun wrists with iron fingers. His other hand lashed out and caught the Yaqui a smashing blow in the face. He reeled back, spouting blood from mouth and nose. Walt lunged a second time, missed, and the two went to the ground together, striking, kicking, gouging. Walt still clamped the man's gun hand as the frantically working fingers pulled trigger again and again. He whirled the other over just as a wild clashing of hoofs sounded in his ears.—

'Help, Pedro!' screamed the Yaqui in Spanish.

His voice died in a choking gurgle as Walt's fist crashed between his eyes; his big body went limp.

Walt flipped over on his side, jerking one of his own Colts from where it was thrust loosely in the Indian's belt. He flung it up as a horseman loomed gigantic against the moon. A gun blazed and a slug spatted dirt into his face. Then the Ranger's six streamed long lances of fire that seemed to centre on the breast of the mounted man.

The frantic horse reared high and Walt saw, against the blue-silver sky, a reeling form that slewed sideways and crashed to earth. The riderless bronk pounded off through the night. His rider lay silent and motionless where he had fallen.

Walt got to his feet, a trifle shakily. A glance told him that the rider of the horse was dead. He turned to the unconscious Yaqui, ripped the *serape* from about his shoulders and quickly bound him with strips torn from the tough blanket. Then he gave his attention to the body of the horseman.

The streaming moonlight showed, when Walt turned him over, a dark Spanish face with high cheekbones framed in lank black hair. The Mexican, for such he was, doubtless had his share of Yaqui blood, but it did not show particularly in his features. Search of his pockets revealed little of interest save a folded scrap of paper. Walt unfolded it, struck a match and read, 'Montgomery, Albemarle.' Walt knew Albemarle to be a county-seat about forty miles to the north. He carefully stowed the paper away and turned to the Yaqui, but found nothing of value except a ponderous key. Then he strode to the locked cabin, from which arose a squealing uproar. He pounded on the door with his fist.

'Shet up in there!' he roared. 'I don't wanta hear no more racket outa you!'

He was not at all sure that the words were understood; but the tone of his voice was unmistakable. The squealing died to a low, wailing murmur. He shouted again and that, too, ceased. It took him but a moment to ascertain that the key fitted the big padlock. He did not, however, open the door. Instead

165

he strode to the bound Yaqui, who was still unconscious, carried him to the cabin and laid him against the wall in the shade of the tree. Confident that the man could not free himself, he tied a gag loosely in his mouth and with a final glance at the dead Mexican hurried to the thicket where he had left his horse. Mounting, he rode swiftly for the Lazy W ranchhouse.

It still lacked several hours till dawn when he reached it, but he did not hesitate to awaken old Jake and Burley Gardner. Burley, his arm in a sling and tightly bound across his chest, was able to ride now and was chafing with enforced inaction. Both old cowboys stared in astonishment at Walt.

'Been hittin' 'em up over to Laska?' squealed Burley irritably, rubbing his bald head and blinking at the light. 'Yuh're a sight! That's the us'al result of Bull Barty's hooch. You young squirts won't never larn nothin' till yuh're so old it don't do no good!'

'Shet up, Burley,' said Jake. 'Walt ain't drunk and he's got somethin' 'portant on his mind. What's up, feller, another drygulchin'?'

Walt was swabbing dried blood from his creased side with a wet towel. 'Not jest 'zactly,' he told Jake, 'but results was sorta the same. I done found Burley's devils!'

Old Jake let out a dismal wail. 'You was right, you onion-haided coot,' he told Burley. 'He's pickled as a pelican.'

Walt grinned at them. 'Ain't had a snort

166

t'day,' he denied. 'Burley's devil was jest a Chinaman!'

Gardner pig-whistled with indignation. 'Chinamen don't hev tails and wings!' he squealed.

'Nope,' agreed Walt, 'they don't; but they wear their hair in a sorta pigtail with strips of silk braided in it to make it longer. That would stick out behind him when he run and with it gettin' dark would look sorta like a tail; and them loose, flappin' sleeves might look kinda like wings, pertickler to a elderly gent who'd packed away a bottle or two!'

Burley squeaked angrily but forgot his indignation in interest as Walt unfolded his story. Both punchers voiced profane amazement when he had finished. Walt was fumbling beneath a cunningly arranged flap on the inside of his shirt. He drew something forth and held it in the palm of his hand. His face was grave.

'I callate you boys has been sorta curious as to who I was and where I come from, even if you was too p'lite to say so,' he remarked. 'Well, I callate this'll sorta 'splain things.'

He held out his open hand. Something glittered on the sinewy palm.

Jake and Burley stared at the shining silver star set on a silver circle.

'Good gosh! be you a Ranger?' squeaked the latter. Old Jake did not appear particularly surprised.

'I'd mighta knowed it,' he said. 'I've seed sev'ral of them fellers and yuh're jest like 'em and do things like they do. Callate yuh're up here to see 'bout that other Ranger feller what got stuck in the back?'

Walt nodded grimly. 'Uh-huh, and I've decided there's a passel of other things what need seein' 'bout, too. Now I want you boys to help me. I'll 'splain things to Miss Betty and I'm plumb shore she'll be 'greeable. There ain't much to do 'round the ranch for the next week or so and it's to ev'body's int'rest here to have that outfit of hell raisers, whoever they are, busted up. I want you to hitch up that old covered wagon in the barn and drive over there and load them Chinamen inter it. Take that Yaqui, too. The Chinamen won't kick up no rukus and the Yaqui is tied. Take 'em down the Sanlucar Trail till you can cut 'crost the desert to Franklin. D'liver 'em to Ranger headquarters there. I'll write you a letter to Cap. Tom McDonough. Smugglin' Chinamen inter the country is 'gainst the law, you know, and a darn, good payin' bus'ness. Looks like the outfit what's workin' here don't miss no bets a-tall.'

Soon afterward the wagon rumbled away through the dark. Walt, after grabbing a bite to eat and leaving a note of partial explanation for Betty Weston, again saddled up and rode north.

Noon found him at Albemarle, a straggling

168

cow town close to the New Mexican border. He hunted up the sheriff of the county, a taciturn old frontiersman, showed his badge and asked a few questions.

'Yeah, I know John Montgomery,' replied the peace officer. 'Don't know much 'bout him, though. Sorta shiftless. Owns a little spread east o' here. Sanlucar Trail runs 'crost it. Don't do much with his cattle but allus seems to have money. What's he been doin' now?'

They talked a little longer and the sheriff left the office. Shortly he was back.

'I talked with the postmaster,' he said. 'Seems Montgomery sends quite a few letters to a party in Laska named Peter Crane. Gets a letter from there, too, now and then.'

Dusty, tired, gaunt-eyed from lack of sleep, Walt got back to the Lazy W well after dark. He cared for his horse and headed for the ranchhouse kitchen. He was reaching for the door knob when the rumble of a voice caused him to pause. He recognized Bull Barty's deep bass.

'Now what's that jigger doin' here?' he wondered. As he hesitated whether to enter, Barty's words came to him plainly.

'Why don't you let me give you the money to straighten the place out, Betty?' he said. 'Ev'thin' I got'll be yores 'fore long anyhow. It would save you all this worry and bother.'

Then the girl's voice, softly caressing—

169

'I know it would, Clarke, but you know how I feel about the old place. It's a matter of pride with me to get it all paid for and free on my own account. Dad trusted me to run things while he was away, young as I was, and that trust has become somewhat of a sacred thing since he never came back. I feel that I owe it to his memory to make good on my own account. You understand, don't you dear? It won't take long, now, the way things are picking up since I hired my new foreman. We'll be married soon, dear—you know I won't put you off. But just let me do this first.'

Walt heard Barty sigh resignedly. 'All right,' he said. 'I've done arranged to sell my place and get outa the saloon bus'ness—ain't no business for a married man. Callate I can buy the Humphrey spread over east of the Lazy W. That'll give us a purty nice outfit. By the way, has Watt Rice been pesterin' 'round here any more of late?'

Walt Lee went softly back to the bunkhouse and sat down to wait until Barty had gone.

'Now if this don't beat hell!' he remarked to the quiet dark.

His strangely colored eyes brooding, his grim jaw set tight, he sat staring at nothing, the slim, steely finger of one hand fumbling a fragment of rough quartzrock, in which beads of gold glowed like drops of slow-oozing blood.

CHAPTER TWENTY-TWO

DEATH IN THE DARK

First pledging her to silence, Walt revealed his Ranger connection to Betty Weston. She stared at him in wide-eyed awe at first, then smiled a trifle wistfully.

'I'll hate to lose my foreman,' she said, 'but I suppose there is no help for it.'

'The way this mess 'round here looks, I won't be leavin' anyways soon,' Walt assured her grimly.

He rode into Laska in the early afternoon and went straight to the postoffice.

'I heerd tell there's a feller in town by the name of Peter Crane,' he told the postmaster. 'You any idea where I can find him?'

The postmaster thought a moment. 'Peter Crane,' he repeated. 'Peter Crane—I know that name. Le'ssee now. Oh, I got it. Nope, I don't know the feller, but he works for the Monarch Mine. When Cooper's man comes for the mail he takes along any what's addressed to Crane. Been up there for a year or more, I reckon. Must work in the office or somethin'.'

Walt thanked him and after a moment's indecision, walked up the hill to the gaunt buildings of the Monarch. Perley Cooper was in his office and Walt was admitted without delay. He went directly to the point, laying his badge on the mine owner's desk. Cooper stared at it in surprise.

'From what I've heerd tell of you, I callate you'll be willin' to give me what help you can and not talk 'bout it,' he told the mine owner. 'Nacherly it's to yore int'rest to have law and order in this community.'

'It certainly is,' Cooper agreed emphatically. 'I have worked darn hard for it for quite a spell—ain't seemed to make much headway, though. Yeah, you can depend on me, Lee. What can I do for you right now?'

'Tell me what you know 'bout a feller what works for you, and where I can locate him— feller by the name of Peter Crane.'

Perley Cooper's black eyes flickered. His lips clucked under his white beard.

'Now if that don't beat hell!' he exclaimed in a disappointed voice. 'Pete Crane was a watchman here. He quit jest last week and pulled out. Nope, I ain't no idea where he went. Un'stand he left town and headed south. In Mexico now, the chances are. You have somethin' on him?'

'I callate he was one of the outfit I'm tryin' to run down,' Walt replied evasively, it being against his principles to reveal more than was absolutely necessary of his affairs to anyone.

'Anythin' else I can do?' asked Cooper. 'Have a drink 'fore you go. By the way, how'd you like to look my diggin's over? I got all the latest minin' machinery installed and my stamp mill's right up to date. Mebbe you're int'rested in sich things?'

Walt was. He had studied mining engineering during his years in college. He hesitated a moment, then accepted Cooper's invitation.

'I'll get my superintendent,' said Cooper, rising. 'He'll show you ev'thin', inside and out.'

The superintendent arrived shortly, an alert young man with a pleasant face. Cooper introduced Walt as 'a rider for a friend of mine.' The superintendent, whose name was Ellington, took Walt in tow and was evidently pleased when the Ranger evinced knowledge of mining problems. He grew somewhat confidential as the acquaintanceship progressed.

'Yes, it is an excellent plant,' he admitted. 'All the very latest equipment, but between you and me, the output does not warrant it. We are little more than breaking even and have been for the past two years. The cost of the investment is too great. The vein was quite rich at first and Mr. Cooper made the usual mistake of thinking it would continue so. It did not. It has settled down to a normal good output but nothing sensational. Mr. Cooper put nearly all of what he took out of the mine during the first two years right back into this costly equipment. In time, of course, he will make money, providing something does not happen to the lode, but it would have been wiser to operate on a more modest basis.'

He paused beside a small building with heavy steel doors. An armed guard lounged before it, rifle ready to hand. He opened the doors, however, at the superintendent's order. Walt peered at the rows of dull-colored ingots.

'That's the shipment we're getting ready,' Ellington said. He lowered his voice so that the guard could not overhear. 'It leaves here day after tomorrow, the fifteenth,' he said. 'We ship by stage, of course, and keep the date secret. Each day a strongbox goes on the stage in the care of armed guards. Nobody can tell whether the box contains a shipment or not. That's a scheme of the Express Company's to safeguard it. The mine is insured against loss, of course. The Express Company would be the loser if anything happened. Well, I guess we'd better go below ground now. You've seen about everything above.'

Through endless, shadowy galleries they trudged. Far above their heads extended a web of interlocked timbers that held the sides of the gutted lode apart. Lights twinkled among the gaunt timbers, which resembled the cleanly picked bones of some giant skeleton. Men were working side veins on the various levels, Ellington explained.

'We might as well start back, now,' he said, some time later. 'The rest is just a repetition of

174

what we have seen.' He talked entertainingly as they travelled toward the shaft cage that would whisk them to the surface again. Walt said little, as was customary with him, but his keen eyes missed nothing. It was the highly developed sixth sense of the man who has for years ridden stirrup to stirrup with danger that suddenly sent his glance up and ahead.

With a mighty sweep of his long arm he sent Ellington careening a score of feet down the gallery. In the same instant the passage rocked and trembled to the roar of a terrific explosion. Down from the shadows above their heads rushed a thundering, crashing mass of shattered timbers and splintered stone.

CHAPTER TWENTY-THREE

THE GOOD MADMAN

Gasping for breath, coughing the dust from his lungs, Walt Lee staggered to his feet from where he had been hurled by the concussion. Had his coordination of brain and muscle been an iota less perfect, they would have been crushed to powder by the avalanche. The flash of the explosion, far up amid the timbers, had been his sole warning. He helped the half stunned superintendent to his feet.

Ellington boiled profanity as soon as he had

recovered sufficient breath.

'Of all the asinine things to do!' he raged. 'Set off a blast that near the edge of the level! It's a wonder they didn't bring the whole mountain down on our heads! Just wait until I learn who was responsible for this!'

They shot up to the level in question and the cage had hardly paused before he was storming along the gallery. A scene of wild confusion prevailed there.

'It must have been a forgotten charge that did not go off when the main bore was driven, sir,' declared the drift foreman. 'There has been no blast tamped here for weeks. The rooms along here are all worked out.'

Finally the super was forced to give it up. Still growling, he led the way to the outer air. Walt Lee made little comment, but he was very thoughtful as he walked down the hill to the town.

Bull Barty was standing in front of the El Dorado as the Ranger passed. He glanced keenly at him with his yellow eyes.

'Saw you goin' up the hill to the Monarch a while back,' he remarked. 'Ev'thin' all right up there?'

'So-so,' Walt told him. He was still thoughtful when he rode out of town.

The following day he again rode the Sanlucar Trail. He felt sure that the snaky track was tied up with the mystery of Curt Gordon's murder and the other sinister happenings in the district. He rode it where the crescent of the hills turned south across the desert, alert, watchful, eyes and ears missing nothing. He had encountered nothing of import, however, when, in the later afternoon, he heard the slow beat of hoofs around a turn. Halting Goldy in the shadow of a thicket he waited, lounging carelessly in the saddle. Around the turn came an ancient Mexican astride a decrepit horse. The old man bowed courteously to the Ranger.

'*Buenos dias*,' Walt greeted him. 'Where you headin' for so late?'

'I take food to *El Bueno Loco Hombre, senor*,' replied the old man, patting a plump sack that rested in front of his patched saddle.

'"The Good Crazy Man!"' Walt repeated wonderingly.

'*Si*,' replied the other. 'He is very kind. Also he has the much skill with medicine and the treating of hurts. We of the river villages bring him food in payment. He lives in the small box *canon* just beyond the next turn.'

Walt glanced up at the overcast sky from which came an occasional mutter of thunder.

'He got a cabin?' he asked. 'You reckon he'd put me up for the night? Looks like it's gonna storm bad 'fore long.'

'Assuredly he will,' replied the Mexican. 'If you will but follow me, *senor*, I will lead you to him.'

The cabin sat in a grove near a little stream.

177

It was cunningly built of notched logs, the chinks plastered with mud. A leanto porch was ingeniously bound in place with withes. On the front was a roomy home-made chair, also bound together with withes. In the doorway stood a little old man with a pleasant, bearded face and soft brown eyes whose expression was perplexedly vacant. He nodded to Walt in a friendly fashion and addressed the old man as 'Manuel.' They entered at his invitation. A fire burned on the hearth and there was an appetizing smell of cooking food. A table, several chairs and a couple of bunks with neatly spread blankets completed the furnishings.

And, Walt noted with increasing surprise, each piece of furniture, including the bunks, was fastened together by means of withes. The old man interpreted his glance and a somber expression shadowed his vacant, kindly eyes.

'Yeah, I tie all my things,' he said. 'I never nail 'em. There's somethin' terrible 'bout nails—they do awful things to folks.'

'How's that?' Walt asked wonderingly.

'I don't jest know for sure,' muttered the old-timer. 'I can't seem to rec'lect, but it's awful.' He glanced up apprehensively as the thunder rolled hollowly between the canyon walls and rain began to patter on the leaves.

'Nails and storms,' he whispered. 'They seem to sorta go t'gether—somethin' awful. I—I can't quite see it—not quite. It was durin'

178

a storm—and the nail—'

He broke off, staring perplexedly. The Mexican glanced significantly at Walt.

'I have brought food, good food, *padre*,' he said gently, drawing the sack forward.

The old man's face brightened, the perplexed stare left his eyes, leaving them soft and kindly.

'I got a fine big kettle o' stew goin' here, too,' he exclaimed. 'Plenty for all of us—had a sorta hunch I'd have vis'tors t'day. Pull up yore chairs while I rustle some plates.'

As they ate he turned to Walt and spoke in normal tones. 'Reckon you think I'm kinda queer,' he said. 'I am, at times, can't help it. Somethin' musta happened to me a while back. I been here three, four years now, best as I can figger it, but I can't rec'lect a thing before that. Don't know how I got here, or when. Don't even remember buildin' this cabin and the stuff in it. Funny, ain't it?'

'I got a notion you musta got bad hurt some time,' Walt told him gravely. 'That mighta destroyed yore mem'ry.'

'I think so too,' said the old man. 'See, I got a purty bad scar here.'

He turned his head to show where, high up near the crown, there was a patch where no hair grew, a patch about the size of a silver dollar. The scalp was livid in color.

'Pahdon me a moment,' Walt said. Reaching over he felt of the scar with his slim, sensitive

179

fingers.

'Jest as I figgered,' he said. 'There's quite a depression there. I betcha the bone is pressin' on yore brain. A good doctor could op'rate, lift it up and I betcha you'd get yore mem'ry back and be all right again. It's been done, lots of times. Ain't you ever thought of it?'

'Yeah, I have,' the old man admitted, 'but I've allus been sorta scared to leave this place. I might get another blank and no tellin' where I'd go or what I'd do. I don't see anybody but the Mexicans from the river village and they don't know much 'bout sich things.'

Walt nodded thoughtfully. 'I gotta move on come mawnin', but I'll be back here in a few days and have 'nother talk with you,' he told the old man.

After eating they smoked by the fire, while the thunder boomed between the canyon walls and the level lances of the rain lashed the cabin roof.

Walt fished into his shirt pocket for a spare sack of tobacco and in doing so spilled the piece of quartz he carried there onto the floor. It bounded across the hearth and stopped at the old man's feet. The result was weirdly remarkable.

The old man stared at the bit of gold ore with dilated eyes. He shrank away from it as if it were a venomous snake.

'Gold!' he mumbled. 'There was gold when he did it! Gold like that! Gold when he druv

180

the nail!'

'Drove a nail where?' demanded the Ranger. The old man's voice rose in a cracked shriek.

'Inter his haid!' he screeched. 'Inter the pore sleepin' feller's haid! He druv it with a hammer! Inter his haid!'

Foam flecked his lips. He half rose from his chair, eyes glaring, and pitched forward in a fit. Walt caught him before he plunged into the fire.

With the Mexican's aid, Walt got the old fellow into bed. The following morning he appeared all right and had apparently forgotten all about the previous evening's excitement. He did remember, however, Walt's promise to return in a few days.

The concentration furrow was deep between the Ranger's black brows as he rode out of the canyon and headed for Laska.

CHAPTER TWENTY-FOUR

ROBBERS' ROOST

The Laska stage station was situated near the Monarch and the Blue Peter mines. The big stage, which plied between Laska and the railroad town to the north, was drawn by four horses, the extra team being necessary because of the coach's construction.

Its sides were reinforced by boiler-plate iron and there were steel slides that could be drawn across the windows, leaving only narrow loopholes through which the inner guard could fire. There was also a shield which offered good protection to both driver and outer guards, of which there were two always on duty.

The coach was the answer of the express company to the costly robberies of the past two years. It was a fortress on wheels and deemed practically impervious to attack.

No chances were taken, however. Only high officials of the mines and the express company knew when a gold shipment was carried by the vehicle. Each and every day the guards rode the stage, and each and every day a heavy iron strongbox was loaded into the stage. One day of the month, possibly two, the box would contain ingots of gold from the mines. On other days it would be loaded with rocks or lead bars. The guards never knew what they were guarding; the stage officials themselves did not know when the gold was shipped. The pleased express officials considered the scheme fool proof.

On the morning of the fifteenth the coach rumbled up to the station. There was a wild flurry of hoofs, an uproar of cursing and shouting on the part of sweating hostlers who led forth the four prancing, mettlesome horses that would pull the heavy vehicle on the run north. The driver, drawing on his gloves, mounted majestically to his high throne. The grim-faced guards, rifles beside them, shotguns across their knees, took their places. The third guard was already inside the coach. The few passengers were held back by the station master and his assistants. A double line of men with rifles posted themselves between station door and stage.

Between these lines, sweating laborers trundled a heavy box. With many 'heave-hos!' and 'altogethers!' they boosted it into the capacious body of the stage and shoved it into place. The conductor signed his receipt. The passengers were allowed to enter. With a clang the heavy door swung shut and was bolted fast from the inside.

The driver gathered up his reins, winked at the station master and threw a facetiously profane aside to a hostler, who grinned in huge delight at being singled out for attention by 'his high majesty,' and replied in kind. The conductor blew a single mellow note on his horn. There was a shout from the onlookers; the station master raised his hand.

Away from the heads of the prancing horses leaped the hostlers, scrambling for their lives as the iron-shod hoofs rang against the road. Lurching, swaying, rumbling, the huge vehicle shot away from the station in a cloud of dust. Soon it was but a yellowish smudge upon the gray of the trail. A moment later it vanished 'round the shoulder of a tall hill.

'Well,' commented the station master, rubbing his hands together complacently, 'there she went, plumb safe from gents with drygulchin' intentions and sich. Callate we got 'em bufferloed at last.'

A man watching from a window heard the satisfied boast and smiled sardonically.

The trail the stage followed wound sharply through the hills, dipping into hollows, clinging to the mountainsides, with sheer drops into nothing at all close to its outer edge. At times it slithered through groves of hackberry or stubbly thickets of mesquite, ideal spots for holdups, where the guards sat tense and vigilant and the driver slumped low behind his protecting shield. Several miles further on the track wound dizzily up a long slant of mountainside, crawled breathlessly over a towering crest and swooped exultantly down the far side of the rise in a series of sweeping bends and curves. Here driver and guards sighed their relief and relaxed somewhat. For several miles the trail showed white and clear before them, the gradual curves affording scant concealment for any lurkers with intentions upon the coach's cargo. Far below, a silver thread set in banks of emerald, Sinking Creek tumbled on its way to lose itself in the desert sands. A bridge spanned the shallow creek. Its banks were thickly grown with willow and cottonwoods.

'Shore glad to get past them rocks up top the rise,' grunted the driver. 'Hidin' places for all the drygulchers in Texas up there. I allus 'spect to ketch it there—coach jest crawlin' after the pull up the hill, hosses fagged.'

'Uh-huh,' nodded one of the guards. 'I allus feel better after gettin' past there, too; 'specially if I happens to be sittin' outside here. Inside ain't so bad—rifle ball ain't made what can get through that iron. Feller inside is sittin' purty.'

'That's chief reason why this outfit ain't never been tackled,' commented his companion. 'Ain't much use in takin' the trouble to throw down on us fellers on the outside. Might do for us, but what'd it get 'em? Them jiggers is bus'ness men; they don't go 'round murderin' folks for pastime. They aims to make it pay. That's why we—'

Cr-r-r-r-rack!

The guards ducked instinctively; so did the driver. The sound a highpower bullet makes when it yells through the air a few inches above a head is conducive to the immediate lowering of that head.

Thud!

That one slammed into the body of the coach and splattered itself into lead splinters against the solid iron.

Cr-r-r-r-ack! The guards twisted about, dropping their shotguns, grabbing their rifles.

185

They peered up the dusty trail toward the fangs of stone that marked the crest. A faint wisp of smoke drifted up from among the rocks; another bullet thudded against the coach before the report came ringing to their ears. Echoes tossed among the rocks. The guards swore wholeheartedly and commenced banging away at the clump of stone.

'Like hell they don't go 'round murderin' folks for pastime!' stormed one of his optimistic companions. 'What you call this? If that hellion up there gets the range a little better we're gonna be so fulla holes we won't cast a shadder. Get them bronks outa a crawl, can't you, driver!'

The driver was doing his best and the pained and frightened horses were responding nobly. From inside the coach came the excited cries of the passengers, who were being bounced around like peas in a running rooster's crop. The inside guard was bellowing hoarse profanity and trying to draw a bead through the swaying slit of his loophole. He didn't know what it was all about but was firmly resolved to shoot first and ask questions afterward.

'Here they come!' yelled one of the guards suddenly. The driver sputtered curses and leaned over to howl at his horses. The other guard glinted hard eyes behind his rifle sights.

From among the boulders flanking the crest, three men had ridden. They thundered down the trail in the wake of the stage, firing their rifles as they came. The guards returned the fire, but the range was so great that no damage was done on either side.

'Them jaspers is plumb *loco*,' growled one of the guards. 'They oughta know they can't hit nothin' off a hoss this far away. This is the plumb daffiest 'fair I ever got mixed up in!'

His companion was frowning back up the trail with narrowed eyes. He had ceased firing and was muttering to himself under his breath.

'What's eatin' you?' bawled the other.

'I don't like it, that's what,' he grumbled. 'It's all too *damn loco!* We're in for trouble somehow, you jest mark what I tell you.'

The driver, glancing over his shoulder, let out an exultant whoop. 'They ain't ketchin' up!' he chortled. 'We're gonna be 'crost Sinkin' Crik and out on the level in 'nother minute or two. Coupla miles farther ahaid is the Conyaga post. They won't never foller up inter the post, and they ain't gonna ketch us 'fore we get there! Hang on, you pants warmers, we're gonna hit the bridge!'

Directly ahead was Sinking Creek and the heavily timbered bridge that spanned it. The driver expertly guided his flying team between the stout guard rails. The speeding hoofs struck hollow thunder from the floor boards.

Cr-r-rash!

The stage was in the middle of the bridge when the whole structure dipped, swayed and

187

hurtled sideways into the stream to the accompaniment of a prodigious uproar of spluttering timbers. Over went the stage onto its side in four feet of water, the horses a kicking, squealing, drowning tangle. Guards and driver were flung far out into the water and vanished with a terrific splash.

Fortunately for the passengers and inner guard, the door of the coach was uppermost. Spluttering, coughing, swearing, they managed to draw the bolt and fling the heavy door open. Like half-drowned rats scrambling from a sewer they clawed through the narrow opening. The guard swore an appalling and utterly disgusted oath and raised his empty hands in the air.

Lining the banks on either side were masked men with rifles. The outside guards and the driver were standing in four feet of water, hands raised, water dripping from hair and moustache, profanity dripping from their open mouths.

'All right, gents,' sounded a muffled voice from the right bank. 'Jest get busy and claw that strongbox outa the stage. It won't be easy, but there's 'nough of you to do it. Fust, beginnin' on the left, pull yore hardware and drop 'er in the water. Easy, now, we got itchy trigger fingers over here. Driver, you cut loose yore horses 'fore they drown.'

There was nothing to do but obey. The three riders thundered up and joined the

188

riflemen; they too were masked. With seven steady gun muzzles menacing them, the unarmed guards and passengers started to do as they were told. The inside guard was the first to re-enter the coach. He eased his body through the door until only his head and the upper part of his chest was visible. Suddenly he seized the door with both hands and tried desperately to close it.

Cr-r-rack! Thud!

Smoke wisped from the rifle muzzle of the outlaw who had spoken. The daring guard dropped back, a blue hole between his eyes. His body splashed hollowly inside the water filled coach.

'Next gent what tries it gets the same thing,' observed the killer. 'Better hustle that box out 'fore I gets nervous.'

There was no more resistance. With prodigious effort the strongbox was hauled forth and carried to the bank. A pack mule was led from a thicket by one of the outlaws and the box loaded onto its back. The driver, in the meanwhile, had managed to cut loose his struggling horses. One of the outlaws drove them up the trail ahead of the band.

'Won't take long for you fellers to walk to the post,' the leader remarked in parting. 'Then you can get word to Sheriff Rice and tell him to come and chase hisself 'round through the hills some more. He won't find nobody, but it's good exercise and keeps him from gettin' fat.'

Which was precisely what the sheriff did, about six hours later, when he got the word. Where the road topped the rise, the trail of the robbers vanished utterly amid the rocks. Keen eyed frontiersmen among the posse were forced to admit themselves baffled.

'They might as well chased a shadder up a tree,' grunted the chattery bartender who related the details of the holdup to Walt Lee upon the Ranger's arrival in town.

'What's got ev'body puzzled,' he added, 'is how them sidewinders knowed the gold would be on that pertickler stage. Not even the driver and guard knowed whether they was totin' the gold or a box fulla rocks.'

'Uh-huh,' Walt agreed, sipping his drink, 'that *is* puzzlin', damn puzzlin'!'

CHAPTER TWENTY-FIVE

A WHITED SKULL

Along with its numerous saloons, gambling halls and pleasure palaces, Laska boasted a remarkably well equipped hospital. There had been some talk of building a church, but it was decided that a hospital was more in order. Walt hunted up the surgeon in charge and had a talk with him.

'Yes, I imagine it is worth trying,' the surgeon said. 'Of course I am not prepared to say for certain until after I have examined the patient, but from what you tell me, I am of the opinion that there are excellent chances for success. Bring him in and we'll see what we can do.'

Walt did not immediately ride to the queer cabin on the Sanlucar Trail, however. In his keenly analytical mind a thought had taken form—a weird, bizarre thing that as yet wavered on tottery legs; but he was becoming more and more convinced that upon its clarification depended the solution of the problem which confronted him.

'The feller who did *that* is back of Curt Gordon's killin',' he declared stubbornly to himself.

Into the desert he rode, leading a patient little burro burdened with pick and shovel and food. He headed south by west until he reached a spot where a rough cross hewn out of a huge boulder shone white in the moonlight. All about it the sands whispered—whispered of the dark secret that lay beneath their ever shifting surface. Already they were burying the cross, heaping themselves toward the gaunt, outstretched arms. Their hissing voices spoke of what they had seen on a black night of storm, and the leering buttes bore silent witness to the truth they spoke, could the tall Ranger but understand.

But the Dark Rider gave scant heed to their bleak hissings. He made camp, cooked himself a meal, smoked leisurely and then set to his grim task. With pick and shovel he attacked the packed sands. After an ïnterminable period of backbreaking toil he drew forth what he sought—a whited skull!

Above the bleached temple was a small round hole. The Ranger stared at it long and earnestly. Then he placed the grisly relic in a sack and, after filling in the grave once more, wrapped himself in his blankets and went to sleep. Around him the sands hissed sibilant anger, voicing their resentment that an impious hand should probe their dark mysteries.

Walt took the skull to the surgeon at the hospital. A few words of terse explanation and the gleam of the Ranger's star enlisted the medical man's aid. With exquisite care he sawed through the dry bone. His verdict was instant and positive.

'The wound was never made by a bullet,' he declared. 'Yes, it could easily have been made by a nail—a nail driven by a powerful arm backed by nerves of steel, for it must have been driven home with a single blow. Lieutenant Lee, the man who did this deed was a fiend incarnate!'

Later during the day, Walt dropped into the El Dorado. Bull Barty was checking the back bar. Business was slack and a loquacious bartender paused to chat with Walt.

'That's shore a purty watch charm the Boss wears,' Walt remarked at length. 'Imagine it was a piece of ore from his claim, wasn't it?'

The bartender shook his head. 'Naw,' he disclaimed, with the condescension of superior knowledge. 'Bull's diggin's never put out no ore like that. His claim was a pocket claim— nuggets and wire gold; that's quartz. That came from the fust assay of the Monarch lode. It was pow'ful rich in the beginnin', but as they went deeper the rock got harder and the gold content cut down till it waren't nothin' to compare with the surface 'croppin'. Yeah, that doofunny was made from a piece of Monarch ore.'

Walt's feelings as he rode to the Lazy W were a mixture of elation and depression. Everything considered, he could not help but feel glad that suspicion appeared to have been lifted from Bull Barty, whom he couldn't help but like, despite his appallingly ugly face. But it was disheartening to have his carefully worked out theory completely knocked off its feet. It appeared now that the clue he had so depended on, the bit of ore taken from Michael Hubbell's coat pocket, was valueless after all. Hubbell may have been carrying it for years—may have bought or begged it from someone as a souvenir. The motive for his killing might have been something altogether different. Hubbell, the son of a rich man, might have carried a large amount of money in gold coin. Possibly he was killed for that.

Just where the demented old man in the canyon cabin fitted into the picture Walt was not yet sure. He hoped to know soon.

'Anyhow, the little gal gets a break,' he mused, visioning Betty Weston's sweet face. 'Bull and her oughta hit it off fust rate.'

His thoughts shifted to Sheriff Watt Rice and his green eyes grew cold. 'I'd shore like to see how a hunk of that hombre's yaller hair would look after it was off his head a spell!' he muttered.

He found old Jake and Burley Gardner in the bunkhouse when he arrived. They reported the successful completion of their mission. They also brought a letter from Captain Tom McDonough.

'The damn Yaqui won't talk and the Chinks don't know nothin',' wrote Captain Tom. 'Reckon it's up to you, son.'

Walt was confident that the vanishing of the contraband Chinamen, apparently into thin air, would confuse and perhaps frighten the smugglers. Jake and Burley, following his instructions, had carried the dead Mexican away with them and had carefully locked the cabin door after removing their charges. Doubtless the rest of the gang would conclude that the Mexican and the Yaqui had double-crossed them in some manner. This, he hoped, would create dissension in their ranks.

The sheriff failed to trail the stage robbers.

Walt had a theory of his own and proceeded to put it into effect. Late afternoon found him examining the smugglers' cabin from the shelter of a mesquite thicket to which he had carefully made his way. The building was silent and apparently deserted. He could see that the heavy padlock had been smashed.

'Somebody's been here since Jake and Burley, all right,' he nodded.

For a long time he watched and listened. The cabin remained as before, silent and deserted. Birds flew about it and showed no alarm. Nor did those that fluttered in the brush along the trail. Presently a furtive fox drifted like gray smoke out of the mesquite and, after a moment of cautious staring, approached the cabin door and nosed about. After a period of sniffing it sauntered unconcernedly across the canyon until it was within a score of yards of the thicket which sheltered the Ranger. Abruptly it flung up its head, poised like a coiled spring and then streaked away up the canyon.

'Can't fool that feller,' grunted Walt. 'He scented me right away. Woulda scented anybody holed up in that shack the same way and hightailed.'

Confident that the cabin was deserted, he slipped from the thicket and approached the door. It was latched but not locked.

Inside the cabin was nothing that bespoke recent occupancy. Walt began a careful

195

scrutiny of the room.

There was dust on the floor along the walls and in the corners. He grunted with satisfaction as his keen gaze singled out a spot that was singularly free from it. The floor-boards there looked as solid as elsewhere, but a moment of effort with a heavy knife brought one sliding smoothly away from its fellows. The two that flanked it on either side came up as readily; the next two were firm.

Walt peered into the narrow opening. The ground beneath appeared undisturbed. He knelt down and sniffed. To his sensitive nostrils came the faint, elusively different smell of newly turned earth. He chuckled and began digging with one of the boards. It was instantly evident that the earth was loosely packed. He redoubled his efforts and a moment later the board struck something solid. A little groping and prying and he hauled forth a dull-colored, astonishingly heavy metal ingot. Within half an hour later he had a heap of them lying on the cabin floor.

'Uh-huh, reckon that's all,' he nodded, prodding the solid sides of the hole beneath the floor. Going outside, he gathered an armful of rocks, dumped them in the hole and then raked the loose earth over them until the spot looked the same as before. Then he replaced the loose floor-boards, chuckling to himself the while.

There was a ragged blanket on one of the

196

bunks along the wall. He wound it into a rough sack, filled it with ingots and carried them into the thicket where he had lain concealed. After several trips he estimated that he had carried some two hundred pounds of gold from the cabin.

'That makes it, all right,' he decided with satisfaction. 'The shipment was valued at close to fifty thousand dollars. Yeah, that's jest 'bout right.'

Burying the gold was harder than digging it up, but he finally got it done. Then he repaired to the cabin once more and carefully removed all traces of his work. Straightening his aching back, he suddenly froze in an attitude of alert listening. Hoofs were clicking up the trail!

CHAPTER TWENTY-SIX

RUINED HOPES

A glance told Walt that the cabin door was shut as he had found it. Loosening his guns in their sheaths, he waited. The hoofbeats drew nearer, ceased; there was a grumble of voices. Walt slid the big Colts from their holsters. A moment later the door opened and two men stepped into the cabin. One was tall and gangling; stoop-shouldered, with a swarthy, moustached face. His companion was blocky and broad. Walt instantly recognized them as members of Sheriff Rice's posse on the day of their first meeting. He had been told later that both worked on Rice's ranch.

'All right, gents, stand where you are and reach for the sky!'

The Ranger's voice was softly drawling, but there was an edge of steel beneath the softness. For a paralyzed second the two men gaped at him, jaws dropping. Then, as if snapped into action by a single spring, they hurtled away from each other, guns coming out.

Coldly, dispassionately as if shooting at a target, the Dark Rider pulled trigger. His heavy Colts gushed a continuous stream of flame; the thundering reports blended into a drum-roll of roaring sound. The two stage robbers died as they stood, hands clamped on gun butts, muscles tensed for the draw. Walt peered through the smoke at the two silent forms sprawled in grotesque attitudes; then he raced to the open door, still smoking guns jutting forward. Swift hoofs were clattering down the trail. A mounted man, bending low over his horse's neck, vanished around a turn as the Ranger's guns boomed again.

Cursing bitterly under his breath, Walt went back to the cabin. Evidently the third man of the party had remained outside to hold the horses. His escape ruined the Ranger's carefully mapped plan. He had hoped to use the cabin as a lure and trap the entire gang there when they came for the hidden gold. Now the alarm would be spread and the rest of the outfit, including the canny leader who was its brains, would give the cabin a wide berth. Walt doubted if even the possibility that their hoard had been undiscovered would bring them near it at any time in the near future.

The pockets of the dead men showed nothing other than the usual odds and ends punchers carried. Walt carefully closed and latched the door, whistled Goldy from the thicket and rode away.

'Well, that makes three of Rice's outfit gone,' he checked. 'That scantlin' of a jigger was the one Bull Barty called Splinter. The one what tried to down me in the saloon was Whitey Davis and—'

Suddenly he broke off with a whistle. A light flared in his cold eyes; he gave a satisfied exclamation.

'*Now* I know who that drygulcher in Black Rock Canyon reminded me of,' he exulted. 'That jigger was the spit-image of Whitey Davis, only older and a little bigger. Betcha me you he was a brother or somethin' to Davis! No wonder Whitey was on the prod and out to get me, whether or no! Well, that makes *four*—six, includin' the Mexican and the Yaqui. Come to think of it, them rustlin' Yaquis I downed mighta been in the tie-up, too. Countin' them as part of the outfit, and with the sheriff at Albemarle holdin' John Montgomery in the jug, she totals up to leven. Well, if they ain't got all Texas and Mexico signed on, the outfit oughta be gettin' purty well thinned down. Now if I can jest drap a loop on that jigger called Peter Crane! I got a notion he could shell out some mighty val'ble information. Think I'll jest ride straight for Laska and see if there's anythin' turned up consarnin' him.'

Laska was boiling with a payday celebration. The streets were a riot of color and noise, the saloons crowded. He visited the postoffice and learned that a letter addressed to Peter Crane had been refused by the Monarch Mine messenger and returned. Walt cursed Perley Cooper's stupidity—and his own neglect at not having arranged to have Crane's mail held at the office.

'Never callated he'd pull out 'thout notifyin' the rest of the outfit,' Walt growled to himself. 'Well, I missed a bet there, that's all.'

He could not locate Cooper, but later in the evening he encountered Ellington, the Monarch superintendent.

Ellington was off duty and had been aiding in the payday celebration. He was not too drunk to talk intelligently, however. He greeted Walt as a long lost brother and insisted on a drink. Leaning on the bar, Walt asked a casual question—

'Ever hear anythin' more 'bout that feller

Crane what left yore place a while back?'

Ellington stared at him a trifle blearily. 'What feller Crane?' he demanded.

'Peter Crane, what used to work for the Monarch as a watchman,' Walt explained. 'Was with you for a year or more.'

Ellington shook his head positively. 'Musta been a couple other fellows,' he replied. 'Nobody by the name of Peter Crane worked for us since I've been here, nearly three years. Nope, we never had a watchman by the name of Peter Crane.'

CHAPTER TWENTY-SEVEN

'THAT'S THE MAN!'

Walt found a visitor awaiting him when he reached the Lazy W ranchhouse. It was the old sheriff from Albemarle.

'Yeah, I got Montgomery jugged,' the sheriff said. 'I callate he told me all he knows, but he don't know much. He's jest a link in a long chain—his place is a sorta way station for the smuggling trains; they feeds and waters the Chinks there on their way nawth. Montgomery assed 'em on to a feller on the New Mexico side. We got his name and the sheriff up there grabbed him—'spects to get the name of the next jigger in line and so on. None of them fellers know anythin' much. Montgomery got orders from the feller named Crane down here. He'd let Crane know when a batch passed through. Yeah, I got that letter he wrote Crane—the one what come back. All it said was the last batch expected hadn't come through on schedule—wanted to know when it would. Montgomery's been in the bus'ness for nigh onto two years, now. Ganglin' feller he knowed as "Splinter" hired him.'

'Splinter won't hire anybody else,' Walt remarked grimly. 'I got headquarters at Franklin workin' on the Mexican end of the bus'ness,' he added. 'It's a reg'lar underground railroad like they had back in slave days to get the slaves up nawth. Ev'dently been goin' on for a long time.'

'"There ain't no law west of the Pecos,"' quoted the sheriff. 'Folks has been sayin' that for many a year.'

'There's law now,' Walt told him, *Ranger law!'*

'So I callate,' agreed the sheriff, 'and I reckon a lot of other gents is beginnin' to think the same thing.'

For long after the sheriff had gone to bed, Walt sat by the bunkhouse window, thinking. One by one, he carefully went over the events that had taken place since his arrival in the district. He paused on the drygulching in Black Rock Canyon, the shooting in the El Dorado saloon and the dynamite explosion in the

Monarch mine. On each occasion he had escaped with his life by the narrowest of margins. His green eyes glowed as he pondered and his stern face was bleak. He checked other incidents, some of them small, some looming large, but all weaving together in a dark and sinister pattern. So far, the master thread by which the whole could be unravelled had eluded him. Now, however, he was beginning to see its elusive shadow coiling through the highlights and the shadows. A theory was beginning to take form in his mind, a startling theory that as yet was nebulous but which grew clearer of form and outline as he catalogued apparently unimportant incidents and saw where one dovetailed smoothly with another. And as he marshalled the facts in his keenly analytical mind, his slim fingers caressed the butt of the heavy Smith & Wesson snugged in the shoulder holster under his left arm—Curt Gordon's gun, the gun of vengeance!

Early morning found him riding the Sanlucar Trail where it wound through the crescent of the hills. He led a spare horse. Early afternoon of the next day found him riding into Laska, stained with the dust of travel. Beside him rode an old man with a gray beard and mild, uncertain brown eyes. They had a bite to eat at a restaurant and then sauntered to the El Dorado for a drink.

'Seems puhfectly nacherel to walk in and

order a drink,' remarked the oldtimer, 'but for the life of me I can't rec'lect ever doin' it before.'

'I got a notion that 'fore long you're gonna rec'lect lots of things you been forgettin' the past four years,' Walt told him gently. 'The doctor is plumb op'mistic 'bout yore case.'

They ordered their drinks and leaned on the bar, Walt sweeping the big room with his keen glance. He noticed Bull Barty in a far corner, talking earnestly with Sheriff Watt Rice. Other faces, grown familiar during his weeks in the district, passed before his eyes. He nodded to one or two acquaintances. His head snapped around at the sound of a choked gasp from his companion.

The old man was staring into the mirror of the back bar, his eyes dilated, his face drawn and gray.

'What's the matter, Dad?' Walt asked anxiously. The old man dripped a whisper over his stiff lips—

'It's *him!*'

'Him? Who? What you mean?'

'It's *him!*' repeated the oldster. '*The feller what druv the nail!*'

Quickly Walt followed the oldtimer's stare. His own bleak gaze centered on the face of the man reflected in the mirror, a man who, unconscious of what was going on at the bar, continued to converse easily with another who lent an attentive ear.

'It's him!' sighed the oldster in a thin, reedy sort of voice. *'He's older, but it's him!'*

The bartender suddenly banged a bottle and glasses on the bar at his elbow. The old man, started as one who snaps out of a bad dream, passed his hands nervously across his eyes and blinked. The face in the mirror had vanished, its owner having moved to another part of the room. The old man's eyes were again mildly vacant and he had apparently forgotten all about the incident. He poured his whiskey into a glass and sipped it with evident relish.

But Walt Lee's glass remained empty on the bar. The Dark Rider's green eyes were a-crawl with smoky flame, his lean jaw was set like iron. The slim fingers of one powerful hand twined about the long strand of hair that lay coiled in an inner pocket. He drew it forth, glanced at it, nodded with perfect understanding.

'The very thing I'd never thought of,' he muttered, 'and right before my eyes all the time! It checks—checks plumb perfect. Was the easiest thing in the world to happen in a ruckus, too. And ev'thin' else ties up with it perfect—the things what was beginnin' to look so darn funny. Now to tie up the loose ends!'

He thrust the strand back into his pocket and his hand closed with a mighty grip on the butt of Curt Gordon's gun.

CHAPTER TWENTY-EIGHT

ON THE SANLUCAR TRAIL

Walt took the demented man to the hospital. The surgeon took him in charge, made a brief examination and was more optimistic than ever.

'I feel sure it will be successful,' he told Walt. 'There is undoubtedly an area of pressure. That area rests on a portion of the brain which it has been pretty conclusively proven houses the function of memory. He evidently received a severe blow at some time, resulting in a fracture and the subsequent depression. Shock could easily have deprived him of memory of events previous to his accident. The later depression tended to aggravate the condition. The murder which he undoubtedly witnessed made a terrific impression on his dazed mind, an impression which was tied up with the use of a nail as the deadly weapon. Which explains the effect anything connected with nails has on him. Yes, I am sure that you can rest assured that the old gentleman will come out of the operation with remembrance of past events and a realization of his own identity.'

Walt visited the president of the Laska bank, revealed his Ranger connections and had a talk with him, at the end of which the president shook hands and promised the interview would be kept secret. He was a bluff old frontiersman who could see through a mill stone when there was a hole in the center.

'I've heerd little things durin' the past coupla years,' he said. 'Things that seemed sorta funny at times. We do bus'ness with that bank, you know, and we learn things. There's been other things come to my 'tention, too. It was darn funny that time we got robbed— mighty few folks knowed when that payroll would get in. Jest as mighty few folks knowed when that gold shipment would be on the stage. Snakes and eagles both get on top of high rocks, you know, and sometimes some mighty ornery spec'mens get inter positions of trust and influence. I don't know jest what you're drivin' at—you ain't said much—but I gotta hunch you'll make the fur fly 'fore yore finished, and for a plumb good reason.'

Later Walt wrote a carefully worded letter to the leading bank in Austin, the state capital. After it was mailed he again took out the strand of hair he had unwound from murdered Curt Gordon's sleeve button. With skillful fingers he wove it into a tiny noose, a noose with a peculiar heavy knot sliding above the loop.

'Not very big and not very strong,' he addressed it, 'but plenty big and plenty strong to hang a slitherin' sidewinder what crawled

207

over a dead man to get on top!'

Walt dropped into the El Dorado during the course of the evening. Bull was busy but had time for a word with the Ranger.

'Jest made a swell deal with Watt Rice,' he told him. 'I been tryin' for some time to buy the Humphrey spread over east of the Lazy W, but Joe Humphrey ain't been so anxious to sell. Callate you don't know it, but me and yore boss, Miss Betty, is figgerin' on gettin' hitched 'fore long. I wanted a ranch 'longside of hers—gettin' outa the saloon bus'ness soon as I'm married. Now long comes Watt Rice jest at the right time and offers to sell me his Flyin' Y, which lies 'longside the Lazy W on the west. I takes him up immediate and we closed the deal this aft'noon. Paid him spot cash on the nail.'

Walt congratulated Bull on the deal and his choice of a wife. Barty glanced around and lowered his voice.

'Watt's been sorta sweet on Betty hisself,' he confided, 'but I callate he finally decided it waren't no go. Reckon he didn't wanta own prop'ty right 'longside hers any more. I wanta thank you, feller,' he added, 'for fixin' things so's we could get hitched so soon. You see, Betty wanted to get her ranch cleared of debt fust. You gettin' them two trail herds t'gether and shipped for her, like you did, got her a nice contract and guaranteed her all she needed to clear the spread; so she's stretchin' a

208

p'int and marryin' me come Friday a week.'

Which information gave Walt something more to think about. 'Is that hellion figgerin' on pullin' out?' he wondered. 'Hell, I can't call a showdown till I get that information from Austin. Little snakes is already under the forked stick, but the noose ain't quite 'round the neck of the big one.'

There followed a series of uneventful days. Tense, expectant days for the Ranger; the information from the Austin bank was slow in coming. He hesitated to spring his trap before it was in his possession. If it proved to be as he expected, it would firmly bind the intricate web of the net he had woven about the suspects. Without it he could not be sure that he had a case that would stand. The word of a demented man, a handful of sawdust and a strand of hair were not much with which to fasten the charge of murder upon a man prominent in a community and firmly entrenched in the good graces of public opinion. The prestige of the Rangers was at stake—and the Rangers were new in this far western district of the 'last frontier.' Here, as elsewhere, Ranger Law must stand the test, must not falter, must be firm and sure in its grip.

There came a night of lashing rain and wailing wind. Wind that screeched down from the frowning summits of the weirdly colored Tonto Hills. It drove the liquid icicles of the rain before it in fierce gusts, the feel of them on the flesh like swiftly flying sleet. Cattle shivered in the lee of cliff and canyon wall. Luckless riders caught in the angry grip of the storm hunched their shoulders forlornly and glowered at the starless sky when they could summon the will to lift their wet faces from the streaming earth. Thunder muttered occasionally and there was an intermittent, wan flicker of lightning that held no promise of warmth.

Through the uproar of the angry elements rode four men. They were lithe sinewy men, dark of feature, hard of eye, with mouths that set in lines of merciless ferocity. The coloring of one was somewhat lighter than that of his companions, his hair was combed back from his forehead instead of falling across it in a square bang, his clothes were the same but his way of wearing them was subtly different. He was apparently the leader and his expression was as sullenly vicious, but lacked the steely strength of his followers.

They rode the snaky windings of the sinister Sanlucar Trail where it slithered between the storm roaring walls of Black Rock Canyon, seemingly indifferent to the beat of biting wind and icy rain. With the sureness of long familiarity they turned up a dizzy track, scrambled their horses over the sawtooth rimrock and sped swiftly across the Lazy W range.

The Lazy W ranchhouse was dark and silent, as was the bunkhouse. Burley Gardner was in Laska, having ridden to the hospital to have his lame shoulder examined. The Mexican woman was in one of the river villages, officiating at the birth of a forty-fifth grandson. The rain battered roof and wall, sluiced from the dripping leaves of the burr oaks, hissed amid the mesquite thickets. Its monotonous pound and the eerie wail of the wind drowned the soft sound of slowly approaching hoofs. Lithe, furtive shadows slipped along the bunkhouse wall. Others loomed for an instant on the veranda steps and vanished in the darkness of the overhanging porch.

The bunkhouse door crashed open. Sudden light blazed. A tall figure, rearing up from a bunk, gun in hand, suddenly sank back under a crashing blow. A knife gleamed, plunged downward.

From the ranchhouse sounded a pound of wet boots, a confused patter, and then, shrill and clear, fraught with utter terror, a woman's scream!

Again shadows sped through the night, and again hoofs sounded, no longer slow and soft, but hammering the sodden range with swift, purposeful beats.

211

CHAPTER TWENTY-NINE

BY THE RIO GRANDE

Walt Lee was in Laska, anxiously awaiting a letter that he felt was long overdue. He looked forward to the morrow, also, the surgeon of the hospital having assured him that the old man would be in shape to receive visitors the following afternoon.

'If the operation is a success, and I feel sure it will be, he should be his normal self again by then,' the doctor said. 'The actual operation is a slight matter. He will be sitting up an hour or so afterward and able to walk about in a few days.'

Things were fairly quiet in the El Dorado, the vicious weather having a depressing effect on the town and keeping people indoors. Walt lounged at a table, talking with Bull Barty. It was well after midnight when he stood up, stretched his long arms and announced his intention of going to bed. He was just turning to the bar for a nightcap when the swinging doors banged open and a sodden, blood-streaked figure reeled into the room. Walt recognized Jake Nesbit.

The old puncher had a huge lump on the side of his head, from which blood was still oozing. Blood drenched the front of his gray shirt. He was breathing in hoarse gasps, his eyes were wild.

'Feller,' he croaked when his gaze fell on the Ranger, 'I was prayin' you'd be here! They got her—they got Betty!'

Walt crossed the room in a bound, supported the old cowboy with an arm and barked questions—

'Who got Betty? What you talkin' 'bout? What happened to you?'

'I'm all right,' panted Nesbit. 'Rode hell for leather, is all. Bump on haid—not bad; little hide slit off my ribs. I had my ol' big silver watch in my shirt pocket—was sleepin' in shirt—and the damn knife glanced off it. Knocked me cold for a minute. Walt, they thought it was you! I heerd one of 'em say in Spanish "*Our* work is done—that fixes the damn Ranger!"'

'What's this all 'bout?' roared Walt. 'I can't make head or tail of what you're sayin'!'

Old Jake got a grip on himself and quickly told of the raid at the ranch. 'They carried Betty off with 'em,' he concluded. 'She was gone when I got to the ranchhouse. Her bed was all mussed up and her coat was gone, too, and some of her clothes. Callate they th'owed 'nough on her to keep her from freezin' in the rain. They headed nawthwest, cuttin' for the Sanlucar Trail, I reckon.'

Bull Barty let out a bellow of anguish. 'We gotta do somethin'!' he wailed. 'What we

213

gonna do, Walt? Didn't Jake say somethin' 'bout you're bein' a Ranger? Gawd, I hope you are!'

'Forget it!' Walt snapped, 'and keep quiet! I wanta think!'

For a tense moment he stood motionless, his strange eyes flaring smokily in his bronzed face. 'They'll head for Mexico,' he said, as if to himself. 'Yeah, they'll do that. They'll follow the Sanlucar 'cause there's less risk of anybody seein' 'em that way. There's a chance, a long shot, but a chance.'

He whirled toward the door. 'Look after Jake, Bull,' he flung back at the saloonkeeper, and was gone.

Old Jake heaved a deep sigh. 'Don'tcha worry none, Barty,' he comforted. 'The little gal'll be back—safe. If you got any worryin' you feel like passin' out free, use it up on them gents what toted her off. They're shore gonna need it!'

Walt saddled Goldy with swift efficiency that permitted no false move. Into the desert fled the great sorrel, south by west, cutting a long chord across the crescent of the hills, a chord whose far end was the rocky straggle of crags where the tip of the crescent reached the banks of the blue-silver Rio Grande.

The rain had ceased but the wind still wailed eerily. All about him the shifting sands hissed and whispered. The grotesque buttes leered and grimaced and at length a watery moon broke through the hurrying veil of the clouds and sent weird shadows straggling across his path. Never heeding, he fled along the unrolling ribbon of the miles like the golden breath of morning. The eastern sky grew pale, turned rose and saffron, shimmered with translucent waves of light. The dawn thundered up over the edge of the world clad in robes of scarlet glory. The Tonto hills flashed a myriad colors. The desert gleamed molten brass edged with silver, and it was day. Before the throats of the birds had spilled their last pearly beads of melody, Walt pulled the tall horse to a halt in a dense grove of burr oaks through which the Sanlucar Trail wound amid a riot of tall grasses and flowering weeds. A glance told him that the quarry had not yet passed this way. If his guess were correct, he was in time.

Working swiftly, he uncoiled his lariat and stretched it taut between two convenient tree trunks on either side of the trail, just at the proper height to send a swiftly moving horse headlong.

'I hope she don't get her neck broke when it happens,' he muttered anxiously thinking of Betty, 'but even that's better than what she's got comin' to her if it don't work.'

Hidden in a thicket he waited with tireless patience, waited until a far away drumming of swift hoofs echoed through the grove. Guns ready, he waited.

Into view burst four horsemen, riding two and two. One of the couple in advance bore in his arms what appeared a shapeless bundle. Without slackening speed they thundered down the trail toward the river's brink.

The leading horse seemed to take unto himself wings when he hit the rope hidden in the tall grass. Walt breathed deep relief as the girl his rider carried was hurled away from the trail and her fall broken by the dense growth of bush. The second horse fell and the following two piled on top of him.

Eyes cold as winter rain, face a gray mask of death, the Dark Rider rode toward the howling welter, both guns roaring. No mercy was to be shown these vicious kidnappers, these who knew nothing of mercy themselves. Shot after shot he hurled at them, his heavy bullets ripping flesh and smashing bone.

But they were fighters, those dark, evil men from the South. They shot Walt's hat from his head, seared his cheek with hot lead and sent blood streaming from a slashed hand. Then they died, three of them instantly. The fourth, the swarthy Mexican, lay retching and gasping, his ghastly face mottled with the sweat of stark agony. The sobbing girl, unhurt but for a few minor scratches, clung to Walt's shoulder as he knelt beside the dying man.

'Might as well come clean 'fore you go, feller,' urged the Ranger. 'Who put you up to this job? Who ordered you to kill me and grab the girl? Yeah, I'll get you water.'

He returned from the river with it in his wide hat, pinching the bullet holes together to keep it from trickling out. The dying man gulped gratefully. He whispered a name, rattled in his throat and was dead. Walt nodded thoughtfully.

'I thought so,' he told the girl. 'Watt Rice was sendin' you inter Mexico. He'll be headin' there hisself *pronto*. C'mon, little lady, fork one of them bronks—the pinto ain't lamed— and hang on. You and me has got to ride!'

Dusk was sifting down from the hilltops when they reached Laska. Without pausing for food or rest, Walt took the girl to the hospital. The surgeon met him, his kindly face wreathed with pleased smiles.

'Perfect!' he exclaimed. 'A perfect success! Memory returned! Knows who he is! Everything! Yes, you can see him at once. By the way, you look as if *you* needed the attention of a doctor.'

The old man was sitting up in bed. His kindly brown eyes were no longer vacant. They were alert, intelligent. Walt threw a long arm around Betty Weston's waist and shoved her toward the white bed. For an instant she stared, the blood draining from her face. Her lips opened in a glad, unbelieving cry—

'Dad!'

'Betty! My little gal!'

Walt Lee grinned at the surgeon and hauled

217

him out of the room. A moment of earnest conversation followed.

'Yes,' the doctor agreed at length. 'Yes, we can take the chance. I don't think it will hurt him. He's strong as an ox.'

There was a letter at the postoffice for Walt. He read the contents with quiet satisfaction. Almost absently, he drew the tiny hair noose from his pocket, shoved the tip of his finger through it and pulled the hangman's-knot tight. Then he sought out Bull Barty, told him the good news and gave him some precise instructions.

Later in the evening, Bull did a strange thing. He slipped through the back door of his building in stocking feet and softly locked the door of one of his private rooms. A little later he sent a trusted messenger to Walt Lee.

CHAPTER THIRTY

THE VENGEANCE GUN

Four men sat in the private room whose back door Bull Barty had locked. Their faces were drawn, anxious, they talked in whispers. Sheriff Watt Rice ran nervous fingers through his golden hair. His two riders, hard-faced, alert men glanced over their shoulders from time to time. The fourth man tried to reassure his companions.

'He don't know a damn thing!' he declared. 'He's jest been gettin' the breaks!'

'Four times we tried to kill him, and four times we failed!' growled Watt Rice. 'What became of that batch of Chinamen, and Pedro and Alqui? Where's Splinter and Walsh? Why don't we hear from Montgomery? I tell you, he's got our number!'

'He don't know nothin' for sure; he's jest had the breaks and he's guessin'!' declared the other man stubbornly. 'I've got another scheme worked out. This time we'll get him. This time we won't fail. We—'

The door suddenly crashed open and the man they were discussing stood framed in the opening. Eyes popping in their heads, jaws sagging, they stared at the tall, menacing figure that lounged easily there, slim fingers hooked over heavy cartridge belt. With effortless ease, Walt Lee glided into the room and a few paces along the wall.

'Gents,' he said quietly, 'it's trail's end. What you doin' here, Cooper?' he drawled with withering sarcasm.

Perley Cooper, First Citizen of Laska, got slowly to his feet. His magnificent white beard rippled over his chest, his black eyes were steady.

'Jest what's the meanin' of all this?' he asked.

Walt gazed at him with an almost friendly

219

expression. 'It means, Cooper,' he said, 'that you've come to the end of yore rope. You crawled mighty high—over a dead man's bones—but you're due to go a bit higher yet—to the drop-trap of a scaffold.'

Sheriff Rice found his voice. 'Jest who the hell are you, anyhow!' he demanded.

Walt's right hand suddenly shot forward. In it gleamed a silver star set on a silver circle. 'Lee of the Rangers,' he said quietly. 'Any other little thing you'd like to know, Sheriff?'

'Oh, Gawd! I know that hellion!' gulped one of Watt Rice's riders. 'That's the Dark Rider, Gawd!'

His bleak gaze again fixed on Perley Cooper. 'Cooper,' he said, 'you're charged with the murder of Michael Hubbell, yore prospectin' pardner of about four years ago. There's charges of smugglin' and robbery 'gainst you other three gents,' he added.

Sheriff Rice went white and his two riders tensed nervously but Perley Cooper laughed with fine scorn.

'You're barkin' up the wrong tree, Lee,' he said. 'Where's yore proof?'

Walt gestured to Bull Barty in the doorway. Bull stepped aside and a man in a hospital wheel chair was shoved forward.

'Here's a witness what saw you drive a nail inter Hubbell's brain,' Wait said softly. 'Here's the man what the Monarch gold strike really b'longs to, the feller what drifted inter your

220

camp with his poke of gold and his location notice that night. You thought he was dead, but he waren't.'

Cooper blanched a trifle, but he still laughed scornfully.

'Fine witness he'd make!' he sneered, 'and you ain't got nothin' on the rest of these boys,' he added, 'nothin' what will stand up in co'ht. Go ahaid, make your arrest. We'll fight you in co'ht, and beat you!'

The smoky flames were back in Walt Lee's green eyes as he slowly shook his head.

'No, Cooper, you won't,' he said softly. 'Fact is, you won't none of you ever be tried on them charges. Cooper, there's somethin' else 'gainst the lot of you!' His hand suddenly shot forward holding a tiny noose of braided hair. 'Cooper, you rec'nize this? You oughta! It's part of yore damn whiskers—a section what got tore loose and wrapped around the button on his coat sleeve when you stuck a knife in a man's back! Perley Cooper, Watt Rice, Ward Turner and Arthur Black, *I arrest you for the murder of Ranger Curt Gordon!*'

For an instant the room was silent as death. Then Perley Cooper's hand moved like flashing light. A long knife gleamed over his shoulder, poised for the throw.

But even as his muscles tensed, Walt Lee flipped Curt Gordon's gun from his shoulder holster. The room roared with the thunder of the report.

221

A blue hole opened between Perley Cooper's eyes. He crashed across the table, blood staining his snowy beard. Watt Rice's gun was out, hurling lead across the room. Walt shot him through the breast and smashed the shoulder of one of the cowboys with a third bullet. The other rider cowered against the table, empty hands held high. Bull Barty seized him, disarmed him and thrust him into a corner, the wounded man beside him. Walt bent over Watt Rice.

The sheriff was going fast. All the bitterness was wiped from his handsome face, leaving it pathetically boyish. His lips flickered in a wan smile.

'Yeah, trail's end, feller,' he whispered. 'I had it comin'. I'd never oughta throwed in with Cooper, but I wanted money damn bad—wanted money and—Betty. I never callated on killin' nobody—jest got in deeper and deeper—started smugglin' Chinamen and 'dobe dollars from Mexico. Then rob'ry, then—murder! Gawd! Yeah, I wanted money, and—Betty!'

He sighed deeply, his eyes closed and he died.

'Well, little lady,' Walt said to the white-faced girl who hovered over the wheel chair, 'well, you're losin' a foreman, but you're gettin' a daddy and a husband, so I guess you'll make out!'

222

                    *   *   *

Days later, Walt sat in Franklin Ranger Headquarters and made his report to Captain Tom McDonough.

'Findin' that plug of dirt in pore Curt's gun started me off,' he said. 'I saw it was sawdust mixed with t'baccer juice. That said for purty near certain that Curt was killed in the saloon, not outside it. His gun dropped inter a spittoon box filled with sawdust, like they allus use in saloons. When I found jest 'bout the same kinda sawdust in that private room in Bull's saloon, I knowed he was killed in that room. Huntin' for hair to match that piece of Cooper's whiskers had me off the trail for a spell. Funny I never thought of whiskers! The minute old Caleb Weston saw Cooper's face in that bar mirror and said he was the jigger what killed Hubbell, I tumbled right away. That was all I needed. Jigger what murdered one man would murder another Cooper's mines hadn't been payin' for years, but the Austin bank statement showed he'd been makin' big deposits right along. That tied the case up proper. Cooper lied 'bout Pete Crane.'

'Why?' asked Cap. Tom.

Walt chuckled. 'Because *he* was Pete Crane. That was plain when his superintendent hadn't never heard of Pete Crane. That explosion in the mine come too pat, too. Ellington couldn'ta been back of it. So who else but

Cooper? He slipped there. Jest like Watt Rice slipped when he come, mad as hops, to the Lazy W to tell me he couldn't find no sign of the dead Yaquis in that mesquite thicket. The bodies mighta been moved, but the signs of the fight woulda been plain for any cattleman that waren't blind. I knowed, right then there was somethin' wrong with Rice. His hair had me int'rested for a while, but it wouldn't match what I carried. Jest like Bull Barty's watch charm. That helped tie things onto Cooper, too, when I learned it was Monarch ore, Findin' ole Cale Weston was luck and helped break the case a lot sooner. It was plumb nacherel to figger he was Betty's father—ev'thin' tied up to show that, time he went away and ev'thin'. Yeah, I got some lucky breaks.'

We hope you have enjoyed this Large Print book. Other Chivers Press or Thorndike Press Large Print books are available at your library or directly from the publishers.

For more information about current and forthcoming titles, please call or write, without obligation, to:

Chivers Press Limited
Windsor Bridge Road
Bath BA2 3AX
England
Tel. (01225) 335336

OR

G.K. Hall & Co.
295 Kennedy Memorial Drive
Waterville
Maine 04901
USA

All our Large Print titles are designed for easy reading, and all our books are made to last.